Warmth and Wit

Blairwriters

ISBN 978-1-291-57246-9

www.blairwriters.co.uk

Blairwriters – 20 years on.

It has been more than ten years since Blairgowrie Writers Group published its first anthology, "Spinning Yarns". The group, which was founded in 1993, became established as a local contact centre for aspiring poets and authors.

Yet another ten years have passed and now the group is named "Blairwriters". New members have joined and others have left, but numbers have always remained constant. The venue changed to Blairgowrie Library and an on-line presence has recently opened the group to a wider following. Members continue to encourage each other and, in so doing, stay true to the group's original aims. It has been an honour for me to lead the group from its infancy to its now well-established position. It has also been a privilege to meet and converse with so many talented and interesting writers over the years.

The Greek origin of the word *anthology* means a gathering together of flowers, as in a garland or bouquet. "Warmth & Wit" will introduce the reader to a variety of writers and their individual styles. The index at the end suggests the range of what you will find: not just poetry and prose, but a delightful mix of characters, experiences and emotions intended to whet your appetite for more. We have categorised our "bouquet" into five themes: Nature; Love & Friendship; Love & Conflict; Local & Scottish; Everything Else.

The decision to compile an anthology is the beginning of a journey, which reaches its destination in the finished product. Or does it? It is my hope that this little book will go further and affect not only the writers and others involved in the process, but the readers too. If our stories or poems encourage someone to put pen to paper (or fingers to keyboard) and attempt creative writing, then "Warmth & Wit" will have achieved its main purpose. Please visit our website at www.blairwriters.co.uk.

I also acknowledge our many debts of gratitude. To artist/illustrator Rosemary Patterson who designed the outstanding cover and category pages, and even found the time to contribute. Thank you, Rosemary. Also, a very special thank you to Ian McGregor of the Scottish Fellowship of Christian Writers, www.sfcw.info, whose advice and expertise was invaluable for the intricacies of getting the book into print and accomplished within a tight deadline. Thank you very much, Ian – we couldn't have done it without you. I would also like to thank the contributors themselves, who submitted their work for consideration and agreed the final selections.

Jane Townsley

Founder of Blairwriters

NATURE

The Thin Place

Heather Innes

Swallows skim the surface of the field
searching for flies in the wet grass
oblivious as we position the camera
and ourselves
for filming.

Our Celtic song reverberates
through these ancient standing stones
and around us
swallows circle dance.

Foxy Lady

Janet McKenzie

By the wild Atlantic breakers, in a den concealed by rocks
Lived a single-parent family with their mother, Mrs Fox.
'Oh Mother, we are hungry,' wailed the little triplet foxes,
'And we all need new trainers and we've holes in our soxes.'

'Oh my darlings!' said their mother as she rummaged
    in her purse,
'Here's enough for chicken nuggets and some fries –
    it could be worse!
But, now you've started playcubs, there's no foxy reason why
I shouldn't find myself a job - at least I'll have a try.'

Next morning at nine-thirty she slunk down to the burroo
But found that jobs for such as she were very, very few.
'I'm not computer literate,' she thought, with some despair,
'I don't know how to drive a van or style and blow-dry hair.'

Then she saw it: *Cleaner needed for the lighthouse –*
    house and light -
Keeper wants his home kept spotless and the lamp kept
    shining bright.
If you're conscientious, willing, and think this job's for you
Then please come to the lighthouse right away for interview.

'This job was made for me! I am uniquely qualified,
But first I'll call in at the den to dress myself,' she cried.
'I haven't any overalls, I must look neat and clean,
White cotton is the answer, hygienic and pristine."

Round her waist she tied the cover of a pillow from her bed,
Then she gathered up the dish towel and wrapped it
        round her head.
Thus be-aproned and be-turbanned, she went for interview,
Got the job without a problem, started it at half-past two.

'My cubs will have their shoes,' she sang, 'my dears will
        have their soxes,
No longer will the neighbours point the finger at us foxes.
The lighthouse keeper rates me high - he almost
        made me blush –
I'm the first and only cleaner to arrive complete with brush!'

Mr Snuffles' Bid For Freedom

Susan Meldrum

"Here I am again – going nowhere!" complained Mr. Snuffles to himself as he went round and round in his little pink ball.

Mr. Snuffles was a ginger and white hamster, owned by Becky, the farmer's daughter, who at that moment was busily cleaning out the cage.

"Now you be good Mr. Snuffles!" trilled Becky, "I'm just going to get fresh water. I won't be long," and she set the plastic ball on top of the kitchen table. Round and round went the hamster, grumbling all the time and wishing he could be free.

Suddenly he noticed a tiny gap in the seam of the ball. Using his sharp little teeth, he gnawed and prised it apart, making a hole just big enough for him to squeeze through.

" I'm free!" he squeaked delightedly, and ran around the table in excitement. But his heart sank when he looked over the edge of the table.

The floor was such a long way down.

"I'll never be able to jump," he thought to himself. "Whatever shall I do?

Just then he heard a clucking sound and who should strut in but Spike, the farmyard cockerel. The back door had been left open, so he had taken his chance to come and have a scout around for any crumbs left on the kitchen floor. Mr. Snuffles saw his chance and wasted no time in taking it!

Spike let out a squawk of alarm as the little hamster landed with a thump on his back. With a great flapping of wings he raced around the table and Mr. Snuffles was tossed into the air, landing in an undignified heap on the floor. As he dusted himself down, Spike screeched to a halt next to him.

"Well! Really-Mr. Snuffles! What are you playing at?" he blustered. "Jumping on me like that! You nearly made my heart stop!"

"I'm so sorry," apologised the hamster, "I had no other way to get off that table." And he explained how he had escaped from his plastic ball.

"I've always wanted to get out of my cage and explore," he said, "but now I'm out...." He gazed nervously around at the towering furniture, "I'm not so sure. Everything looks so big."

By this time Spike had recovered from his fright and he fluffed up his feathers and preened himself.

"Stick with me Snuffles and you'll be just fine!" he crowed. "Come on; I'll show you round my domain."

And putting a protective wing around him, he led the little hamster over to where some cake crumbs had fallen on the floor. They polished those off and had just started on some grapes which Spike had fetched from the fruit bowl, when the door burst open and in raced a tiny field mouse, with Nooka, the tortoiseshell cat in hot pursuit.

Instantly, Spike drew himself up to his full height and stepped in front of Nooka. Flapping his wings, he opened his beak and gave his loudest cock-a-doodle-doo! Momentarily distracted, the cat stopped and turned her emerald green eyes on him. Mr. Snuffles dashed over to the terrified mouse and pushed her under the dishwasher. It was Minnie, one of a big family of mice who lived behind the garage at the back of the house. Mr. Snuffles had often seen them on summer evenings outside the window, and sometimes on cold winter nights she and her brothers and sisters would venture into the warm kitchen to forage for scraps.

"Whew! That was close!" she panted. "Thank you so much Mr. Snuffles, but what are you doing out of your cage?"

"I've escaped," he replied, "and I'm having a day out with Spike."

From the safety of the dishwasher the two little animals watched as Spike strutted around the room, taunting Nooka and daring her to give chase.

"Catch me if you can; fur-ball!" he crowed, and laughed as she hissed and spat. Finally, with claws out-stretched, she made a lunge for him, but Nooka was an old cat, and no match for the crafty, young cockerel. Before she could reach him, he was out the door, and up his favourite tree, singing a rude song!

Realising she had lost, Nooka flicked her tail and flounced away, feigning disinterest.

Mr. Snuffles and Minnie watched the whole show with delight and once the cat was safely out of the way, they came out from under the dishwasher.

"Thank you so much for helping me Mr. Snuffles," said Minnie, politely. "Please come home with me now for some lunch. I know my family would love to meet you. We've often wondered about you."

Mr. Snuffles was delighted to accept, and he had the most wonderful day of his life, accompanying Minnie on the trip across the garden to her cosy little nest. The sounds of the birds and insects, the smells of grass and flowers, the feel of the warm breeze as it ruffled his fur.... Mr. Snuffles could hardly believe such happiness existed. Minnie's family greeted him like a long lost friend, they fed him so much fruit, cheese and nuts that he had to have an after dinner nap, then he played hide and seek and rough and tumble with all the brothers and sisters till it began to get dark.

"We have a short sleep now" explained Minnie, "then we go out collecting food. You can live with us if you like. You're very welcome."

But Mr. Snuffles was beginning to feel a little homesick by this time. He wanted to sleep in his own bed and he missed hearing Becky's soothing voice and her bedtime kiss. He thanked all Minnie's family very kindly and promised to visit them again some other day. As he scurried home across the darkening lawn, he was suddenly scooped up by a small gentle hand. It was Becky – his special friend!

"Oh Mr. Snuffles!" she said joyfully, "I thought I'd lost you for ever! I'm so glad you've come back. Daddy has promised to build an outside run for you, so you can play on the grass whenever you like!"

And as Mr. Snuffles snuggled happily into Becky's neck, he knew he'd made the right decision!

Spring

Barbara Lynch

Spring clean your mind it's nooks and crannies,
From all that's there and lurks around,
You'll be surprised the space it gives you,
You'll be surprised how good it feels,
Just like spring times yearly challenge
To rejuvenate the natural world,
So gather strength from this great wonder,
Spring clean, refresh, renew your mind.

Visit Woodland

Janet McKenzie

Visit woodland - yes today!
Pack a bag, get up and go.
Ditch appointments - don't delay,
catch the great autumnal show.

Overnight the woodlands turn to umber,
orange, scarlet, brown.
All at once the bushes burn,
all at once the leaves come down.

Looping, swooping, falling, stalling,
reeling, wheeling, blazing, amazing!
Earth-wards gliding, thermal riding,
whirling, twirling, senses fazing.

Visit woodland - make it soon!
Join the great autumnal ball.
Leaves dance to the breeze's tune.
Come - succumb to beauty's thrall.

(First published in The Fireside Book 2012)

Weather

Rosemary Patterson

Hot, then cold, then warm again,
Sun and flowers, wind and rain.
Lunch outside in sheltered nook.
Lazy sunshine, with a book,
Sowing seeds, making plans,
Rush to buy some bedding plants.
Then hats and coats and scraping snow,
Icy blasts, north winds blow.
Chopping logs, heating on,
Flowers droop, blooms all gone.
Hot and cold, pain or pleasure,
Up and down, Scottish Weather!

Winter

Annie Johnstone

Winter is blue in eyes specks of ice - flecked sea
Lady Summer has merely glimpsed them from afar
The ink spatters on the pure driven whiteness of

The snow she imagines when it falls to be the
Confetti as they emerge icy, cool in burning hand
Smiles for the camera and they are running

Mr and Mrs Fire and Ice. No more duty, duties
Obligations and laws must be upheld as mistress
Of all things golden she is keeper of the season of

The glow meanwhile Majestic Winter paces that
Shivering cave playing aloof he melts little by little
Night after night unwanted cold and clear images

Of her blazing goddess so full of vibrancy and
Youthful abandon Winter is a realist he knows the
Rules the physics, of what can and cannot be

Silly woman making doe eyes those golden orbs
Are liquefying what needs to be frozen, he hears
Her calling her voice brightly lit from above him ready

To consume him, vaporise his very soul, in a blizzards
Whirl of pain he turns from the heat his back an
Impenetrable stone cold wall Lady Summer lets a tear

Drop and burn her cheek with closed eyes she turns to
The sun Winter steals one last glance skywards and lets
The frost creep in water turns to ice once again

The King and Queen go on
Weighted with wanting

Winter Wishes

Jane Townsley

Thank you for your Winter Wishes
You've been so very kind.
I'm wished a yummy Christmas
With puddings and cakes so fine...

Thank you for the robin
Dressed in his little hat so sweet
He looks so much like Santa Claus
From his head down to his feet

A teddy bear in hat and scarf
Is as cuddly as can be
And how cute the little fairy is
Atop a glistening tree

The snowman has a smiley face
The halls are decked with holly
Pretty stockings by the fire
And Santa looks so jolly.

His sleigh is filled with gifts for us
Reindeer prance around the grot
It seems you have it all prepared -
But is there Someone you forgot?

Thank you for your Winter Wishes
It's clear you wish me well
But I'm unsure what you celebrate
It's rather hard to tell.

It saddens me to think that you
Don't know what Christmas means
Or if you do, it's slipped your mind,
These truthful Christmas scenes -

Scenes of shepherds in a field,
A crowd of angels in the night,
Wise men led to Bethlehem
By a bright star's dazzling light

There, the babe, in swaddling clothes,
In a lowly manger lay.
He is born! And that is why
We call it Christmas day.

A Blow to the Ego

Jessie Nellies

Just retired, and I'd like to keep healthy
So I'm taking a walk every day
That's how I met Sam by the water
Said, "Hello, it's a real bonnie day".

We talked for a bit and he listened
While I grumbled and vented my views
About all who came on the telly
And upset me with depressing news.

Then after two days, feeling friendly,
I said, "Come on back, meet the wife.
She'll have a drink waiting for us
And always a tasty wee bite."

Well she took to Sam in an instant
I could tell by the look on her face.
When he kissed her hand, she was glowing
And said, "Welcome in. Find a space".

Turned out he never had family,
Was making a life on his own.
Well now he's up in the spare room
And making himself fair at home.

With a swanky big bed and new blankets,
He comes and he goes as he please.
All she says is "Hello, Sammy, darling,
Just come here and sit beside me."

They kiss and they cuddle for hours,
She brushes his bonnie black hair.
She uses my very best hairbrush,
Saying, "Wheest! You've got plenty mair."

He's stolen my very best slippers
I got for my birthday this year
And I saw him nick my new jumper
I never had one chance to wear.

I'll not bother saying "I'm hungry",
She'll say, "Look in the fridge and you'll see
There's something in there to tide over
While I get wee Sammy his tea".

So listen you lads to my warning,
Be prepared for some changes in life.
You'll find you're no longer the boss in the house
When you take a dog home to the wife.

Angel Feathers

Jane Townsley

No-one ever knew his name. Some said he was odd, a few colours short of a rainbow but they weren't at church that Sunday when he turned up dressed as an angel.

"Hey Mister," a lad from the nearby housing estate called. "Did ye faa aff the cake?"

"Better than that, young man," he replied, fluttering his wings and sending a shower of green and gold feathers over them both. I won first prize in the Heaven and Earth Fancy Dress at Stardust Nightclub."

"Heaven and what?" Ben looked puzzled but then shrugged. "I wis at a fancy dress once but I didna win."

He recalled Jimmy's birthday party. Jimmy asked to dress up and his mum had obliged with a spider-man outfit. Jimmy's brother had been a frog, and he'd won. Ben hadn't had an outfit, so Jimmy's mum had lent him her denim waistcoat and a yellow bandana. She had told him he was the most handsome cowboy ever. It wasn't true. He wasn't handsome and real cowboys had white hats and spurs but the party had been good. It would be nice to have a mum, Ben thought. Most days he missed his mum but at Jimmy's party, he had missed more than her. He missed being loved.

Jimmy's mum wasn't perfect - she made him go to Sunday school.

"Why aren't you in Sunday school?" the angel asked, as though he could read his mind.

"I did go once," Ben said, "but they didna want me back."

The angel studied him. "Why not?"

"The teacher wis asking aboot the ten commandments and we aa had tae think o yin. I said, "Thou shalt not lie doon aside the green pastors." Mrs Ellis startit laughin and then they aa laughed. Jimmy didna laugh at me though." Ben's face reddened. Finally he admitted, "So I swore at them... an kicked the teacher. I wis telt nivver tae come back. That's how I'm waiting fer Jimmy."

"I see," the angel said. He hitched up his long skirt and adjusted his halo. He nodded towards the church. "Do you think I'll pass?"

Ben was sure the angel's eyes twinkled, and he grinned. "Can I come an watch?" he asked gleefully.

The angel swirled and more feathers, more angel dust, scattered. "Let's go."

Ben's hand was lost in the angel's firm grip. The heavy church doors swung open. Suddenly they were inside the vestibule. The choir had begun the chorus of Hallelujahs and the congregation was struggling to reach the high notes. Mrs Ellis sat closest to them and looked up. Unfortunately, she was in the middle of a particularly ear-piercing octave, which escalated into a scream. All heads turned.

Ben's angel was unflappable. He lifted his wings to full spread and swept down the aisle. Ben stood rooted to the spot. On cue, a beam of sunlight blasted through the stained glass making the wings appear translucent and ethereal. The choir continued their chorus of "Ha-le-lu-jah! Ha-le-lu-jah! Ha...

ha...", before fading to subdued whisperings about irreverence and blasphemy.

Reverend Fairweather, in his pulpit, removed his spectacles. There was silence. In a loud voice, laden with authority, Ben's angel addressed the congregation. "Fear not! I have not come to disrupt this service but to join you in worship." Then he turned and smiled at the minister.

Reverend Fairweather cleared his throat. "Er... Yes, um.. welcome, sir. Please... please sit." He motioned to the empty pew at the front.

The angel made no move but smiled at Ben with pure joy. Ben still stood by the vestibule door. Reverend Fairweather and the congregation followed the angel's gaze. "You too, child. Come in," said the Reverend. As Ben walked slowly down the aisle, the angel pulled in his wings and sat. Ben snuggled close beside him.

The minister began thumbing through his bible. "Yes, well now... Uh... God's house is open to all, no exceptions.... all welcome, so it says... somewhere..." He leafed through the pages while everyone waited.

A moment later, he stood up and drew in his breath.

Somewhere in this action, his composure returned. He stared, his eyes taking in every member of the congregation, including Mrs Ellis and the choir before coming to rest on Ben and his angel. "Our sermon was going to be about the miraculous events surrounding our Lord's ministry but instead I will preach on our Lord's teachings of tolerance, despite our prejudices. I do not use that word lightly.

"Just because someone is different, does that give us the right to reject them? They may dress differently..." He glanced at the angel. "Their behaviour may be... bizarre. They may not follow our home-made rules, and God forbid, they may even break them. We want to shape them into our image. If they won't conform, we conclude that they don't belong. We had rejected their appearance, their background, their language but now we reject *them*. Wha's like us? Aye! Wha's like us?"

The congregation bolted upright as the Reverend suddenly broke into broad Scots and bellowed to the rooftops. "Div we ken wha's like us? If only the answer really wis "gey few", but the truth is: Ower mony! Aye! There's far too many o oor kind. Wha's like us?"

Some members of the congregation were beginning to squirm.

Had Reverend Fairweather lost his mind? They exchanged glances but stayed in their seats.

He went on. "Wee sleekit coorin tim'rous beasties that we are! Verily, verily I say unto youse... Aye! Youse! Wid some power the gift tae gie us to see oorsels as ithers see us. It wad frae monie a blunder free us an foolish notion. What airs in dress and gait wad lea'e us, an ev'n devotion! "

"That's no in the bible, is it?" Mrs Ellis's mother-in-law asked.

"Rabbie Burns," Mrs Ellis whispered.

"Who?" Mrs Robertson had forgotten her hearing aid.

Mrs Ellis shouted, "Rabbie Burns!"

26

"Oh, very good. Carry on, Mister Fairweather." Satisfied she settled back to listen. It was more interesting than most sermons and the Reverend was bellowing so loudly she had no trouble hearing every word.

"Hypocrites! Did the Lord no say that if ye as much as look at a body wi hatred in yer herts, you are guilty o murder?"

Reverend Fairweather roared to the rafters. "Aye! Turn tae the Gospel o Matthew chapter 5 verse 22". The Reverend tore through the pages and found the verse. He quoted, "Ye hiv heard it said, Thou shalt no' kill fer whosoever kills shall be in danger o the judgement. But I say untae you, that whosoever is angry wi his brither withoot cause shall be in danger o the judgement..."

"Is it still Rabbie?" Mrs Robertson asked.

"No. The bible," said Mrs Ellis.

"Sounds like Rabbie tae me!" sniffed Mrs Robertson.

The Reverend broke into a sob, tears pouring from his eyes. A hush descended. Even Mrs Robertson was silent.

The angel stood up and applauded. Ben didn't understand why Mr Fairweather was upset, nor why the angel was clapping, but angels knew stuff, didn't they? So, in faith, Ben started to clap too. A few others joined in and soon the entire congregation was on its feet applauding and cheering. Some were smiling, some were nodding in agreement with the unusual sermon and some were bawling their eyes out. Ben looked towards Mrs Ellis, who had turned pale. Next to her, Mrs Robertson was dabbing at her eyes. Mrs Ellis came forward and gave Ben a soft kindly look.

"Ben?" She whispered his name.

Ben thought she was going to cry too. He waited. She waited.

Everyone waited.

"Aye?"

"Would you please come back to Sunday school? I want you to. I should never have... I'm so sorry, Ben. Please forgive me."

It was strange to hear your Sunday School teacher saying sorry. Ben knew that he should be the one saying sorry. He had kicked her.

"I... uh.. I'm sorry too, Mrs Ellis," Ben choked the words out.

"I should nivver hae kicked ye." He tried not to, but he couldn't stop his eyes filling and before he knew it, he was bawling. Mrs Ellis reached out her arms and Ben fell into her comforting hug.

Reverend Fairweather stepped down from the pulpit and formally welcomed Ben back into the fold. The congregation smiled their approval and continued the applause, this time for Ben and Mrs Ellis. Ben felt a glow inside. It rose up and filled his soul. He remembered this feeling. He'd known it a long time ago. Unconditional love.

It was some minutes before everyone made their way outside. Mrs Robertson first noticed he wasn't there.

"Where'd he go?" said asked. "Couldn't have missed him in that outfit."

Reverend Fairweather went back inside to look but there was no sign of the angel. At least that's what he said.

It was years until he admitted that there had been a sign. A single gold and green feather had fluttered from the rafters and landed at his feet.

Daisy Belle - Our Housekeeper

Joy Dewar

She was a small efficient woman with lovely brown eyes and a bit of a plodder but she did her job well and since she was on a weekly wage there was no hassle to get her to work faster.

She kept her room very tidy and I always thought Daisy (Miss Belle) was a bit of a stick in the mud until I discovered she had an unusual hobby - I might even say an erotic hobby.

Daisy was a vegetarian and was slim and rather bland but behind the quiet, placid exterior there stirred an exciting female - one that no one connected to Daisy Belle. Her hobby was Belly Dancing!

This she entered into with great gusto. She had the veil, the shawl and the gold sandals. Her hip swinging and all other manoeuvres in the class made her a star pupil. No one for one moment would have believed that our quiet housekeeper would indulge in such 'depravity'.

My mother was horrified when she discovered her guilty secret and sacked her on the spot. She didn't want her daughter contaminated by Daisy Belle.

Not that Daisy cared - she eloped with the milk-man and she is probably still enjoying her belly dancing.

Miracle on Christmas Eve

Elizabeth Leslie

'Why am I even *doing* this?' Julie thinks. 'Driving through a snowstorm at midnight on Christmas Eve? I must be mad!'

But she knows she's not mad – just anxious about her Mum. An hour ago she was at Sophie's party, dancing, exchanging gifts, having fun.

Then came the phone call. Her Mum's been fragile since Dad died and tonight she sounded distraught. Julie left the party at once, against the advice of her friends.

'It's snowing hard. You can't drive ten miles through that.'

'It's far too late to set off!'

But Julie was adamant. Her Mum needed her. And she's managing! Only two miles left to go. But the storm is getting worse and she's almost blinded by the flakes dancing in her headlights. Heart racing, hands sweaty on the steering wheel she drives on. Then it happens! As if in slow motion the car starts to skid, does a perfect u-turn and ends up nose first in the shallow snow-filled ditch. The jolt of impact cuts short her scream of terror, but she is shaking uncontrollably with shock. Realising, however, that she's not actually hurt, she switches the engine off and pushes the door hard against the wall of snow. Her dress rips and she loses a shoe as she scrambles from the car.

Shakily she checks her mobile. No signal! Now what? Despite the warm jacket she'd thrown over her light dress, she's shivering with cold and fear.

'Looks like I'll have to start walking. At least it's stopped snowing,' she thinks, then looks ruefully at her feet, one shoeless, the other still in its 3 inch stiletto. Tears run down her face as the reality of her situation hits her. She could freeze to death out here!

Suddenly headlights illuminate the still, white world. A jeep silently approaches, slows down, stops. Limp with relief she greets the young man who jumps out. 'A local farmer, maybe?' she thinks. Warnings about being alone with a stranger in the middle of nowhere flash through her mind, then are quickly dismissed.

'Oh well, he *seems* OK and he does have kind eyes,' she assures herself.

Cutting short her garbled explanation, he expertly attaches tow ropes, climbs into the jeep and slowly pulls the car from the ditch. Within minutes it's back on the road.

'A few bashes to the bodywork, but everything else is fine, you'll get to your Mum's safely now,' he assures her, after giving the car a thorough check.

He waves aside her thanks and wishes her a Happy Christmas.

Then he's gone, the jeep gliding silently off into the night. She stands in the middle of the road and watches its tail lights disappear into the distance.

'Nice guy. A bit mysterious, but thank goodness he came along when he did, and knew what to do. He said I'll get to Mum's safely – *Mum's*? How did he know I going there? I didn't get the length of telling him that – did I?'

Shaking her head in puzzlement, she opens the car door – and her heart skips a beat. On the seat lies a small white feather!

Moving On

Barbara Lynch

The time had come to downsize and what a difficult decision it had been! Although there were many positives in moving, Ruth would dearly miss the old house and garden. It was all too much for her now.

Today was the day she had decided to begin de-cluttering but where would she start? Ruth wandered from room to room, opening cupboard doors and looking along shelves crammed with all manner of things.

When planning the task, Ruth had decided to put her possessions in four lots: bin, recycle, charity and finally things she would keep. She knew she would have to be ruthless, so the sooner she started the better.

She would make small decisions first, she thought and with this in mind, her eyes came to rest on her favourite jewellery box. She reached up and lifted it carefully down from the shelf. She remembered as if it was yesterday. That day back in 1959, she had been given this as a thank you for being bridesmaid at a family wedding. It was made of black lacquered wood and covered in the most wonderful Japanese design. A little ballerina popped up as she opened the lid but the musical mechanism no longer worked. However, Ruth found herself humming the tune it used to play.

She scooped up a silver thistle brooch, its heather coloured gemstone still sparkling after all these years. Ruth could recall being presented with this for being sports champion at her primary school. There had been so many different races: flat race, egg and spoon, needle and thread, obstacle, slow cycle, wheelbarrow, three legged, high and long jump.

For a moment she was back there. She could hear the cheers and laughter of her friends and family, her heart pumping in her chest and her overwhelming determination to do well.

Sports day had always been held on a Saturday afternoon towards the end of June. Strangely, she could only remember the sunny days and how exciting it had been, a family day out with picnic and ice cream to follow.

Now, let's see, Ruth thought, as her fingers, not so nimble now, tried to untangle a little pin type brooch. It had an inscription in an unrecognisable language around the crest and had a tiny aeroplane attached. She smiled as she remembered Alexei, her penpal and first boyfriend. She was the envy of her classmates that year. No, she couldn't possibly part with this.

The doorbell rang. Who could it be?

Ruth quickly returned the jewellery to the box and hurried to the door.

"Hello, Jessie, come away in." Ruth had forgotten she had invited her friend round.

There was always another day to sort through her things, Ruth thought to herself. Spending time with friends was much more enjoyable and anyway, making new memories was just as important as remembering old ones.

"Coffee or tea, Jessie?"

The Last Father's Day

Jane Townsley

Evelyn was waiting at 7 o'clock. In the car, she became very quiet. We were on our way to the cemetery. It had been a chance remark she had made the other day about it being Father's Day on Sunday and how she missed her Dad and the good times they had shared.

"What happened?" I asked and waited expectantly for the sad tale. Instead she looked at me as though I was totally lacking any understanding.

"He died."

That was it. Those two words were more explosive than a thousand. Her sorrow hung in the air between us. I couldn't bear to break the sombre silence.

Eventually Evelyn did. "I used to get him a card but I can't now."

"You can," I said. "Buy him a card and on Sunday I'll take you to the cemetery to give it to him."

"Would you do that, Kate?" she asked, tears filling her eyes.

"Of course," I said, relieved that I could do something, anything to help. I'm like that, especially with Evelyn. I don't know why they call it Down's Syndrome. Evelyn is made for laughter. It's in the way she brightens up a room just by entering it. "Hello," she bellows. "I'm here!" and then her absolute delight in meeting someone she knows. Someone she met yesterday is given the same delighted greeting as life-long friends. Evelyn and joy are rarely separated and the world is a very uncomfortable place the few times that has happened.

So there we were. Father's Day and I was spinning the car out the Main Road and into the cemetery. Evelyn showed me the grave. It was her mother's. Her father's ashes had been scattered over it. She held the card in place with a few white pebbles and used more to weigh down a posy of silk flowers. "I'll leave you alone for a minute," I said. She looked at me quizzically.

"So you can tell him Happy Father's Day and thank him for being your Dad," I explained.

I tried not to listen as I walked away, but it was difficult.

Evelyn's voice carried over the wind.

"I miss you, Dad..."

I wasn't being kind out of any pious sense of duty. My reasons were selfish and simpler. Evelyn's sadness did something to me; it wrenched my insides in some inexplicable way that I couldn't stand. I had to do something to make her smile again. Maybe it was chance, maybe just to put some distance between us, I'm not sure, but I found myself heading towards another grave. My own father's.

I had been twelve when he died. A child, with a child's understanding of life and death and fearful of the vast unprotected unknown that stretched out before me. Now, almost 40 years later, I stood by the grave of a man I never got to know, and I wondered if I too should have brought a card.

An image filled my mind of another Father's Day, excitedly counting out my paper-round money to buy a card and a Commando book. In my neatest handwriting, written with love, and wrapped in joy. So long ago. The last Father's Day. There have been none since. Maybe there should have been.

"Whose grave is that?" Evelyn had appeared beside me.

"That's my Dad," I whispered, then added, "Happy Father's Day."

The Yoga Girl

Elizabeth Leslie

My goodness – that girl's doing her yoga again. Every morning she does it, sitting on the river bank, right across from my kitchen window. Two weeks now since she moored her wee houseboat over there. Not that I know anything about her. *I* keep myself to myself. Too much, Jean says. *She* thinks I need company.

'Mum,' she says in that bossy voice, 'It's too lonely here. Why not apply for a shelter flat in the town? You'd be among people. With a warden in charge.' But what would *I* want with a warden? *This* is my home. Has been since my George and I came here fifty years ago.

Anyway, what's she doing now? I'll just take another wee peek. She's still sitting there, nice-looking lass with that long fair hair. Funny that, she's like someone I've seen in an old photo ….Oh, this'll nag me till I find out. Now where's that old album? It should be in the sideboard drawer. Ah, here we are – let's see. There's Mum and Dad done up all posh for their wedding day. Bless them! And here's me as a wee girl, look at the ringlets! And me at twenty, young and bonnie with my long blonde hair, just like ….just like that yoga girl! Well, I never! And look at me now – old and wrinkled and grumpy-looking.

Ah well, best stop this before I get maudlin. These dishes won't wash themselves. But I wonder if she's lonely. She seems to be there all on her own. Maybe she could do with a friendly word. And there's that baking I did yesterday in case Jean and her man dropped in. They didn't of course. Too busy.

I could take a few scones over to the girl, introduce myself, not be pushy mind, folk don't like that. But - yes, I'll do that.

Well, that Sarah's a *real* tonic! From Australia, too, here for a year. Showed me round her boat, lovely it is, with these fancy coloured cushions and that bright wee kitchen. All mod cons too, even a shower. And these stories about her travels – I nearly choked on my cup of tea I was laughing so much. Then she told me about her yoga. 'Annie,' she say, 'I've started a yoga class in the village hall. Why don't you come?' That set me off again. I mean, with *my knees*? But she said I'd only do what I'm able for. So I've signed up. And she'll run me there and back in her wee car. Then I told her about the photo and she wants to see my album sometime. What a morning – I haven't enjoyed myself so much for ages.

But look at the time – and I *still* haven't done these dishes. Oh well, what's a few dirty dishes when you've just made a new friend?

My Girl

Jill Geary

Precious moments of joy are…
When she holds my hand
When she smiles at me
When she giggles at my tickles
When she asks me to sit next to her
When she does something funny and I laugh
When she wants me to play Barbies
When she asks for my help
When she cries and comes to me
When we sing together
When we play in her Wendy House
When we dance together
When we talk in whispers
When I see her face light up to see me
When I help her learn something new
When I read her a bedtime story
When I tell her I love her and
She tells me she loves me too

love conflict

Gossip

Jessie Nellies

Whit's that ye say? Oh, good mornin,
I jist nivir saw ye oot there.
Ma heid's fu o clouds whin I'm strollin
An takin the fresh mornin air.

No, Ah dinna mind if ye join me
It's grand tae meet somebody new
But dinna fash if Ah'm nosey
An ask a few questions 'boot you.

Whit's that? Ye jist heard a story
This morning, as ye left the kirk.
It wiz causin a bit o a flurry.
Mind, gossip is Lucifer's work.

No, stop lass, please dinna continue
Ah'll hear nae mair o this chant.
I'll niver believe sic a tale's true
A'm sorry fir this angry rant.

I ken the guid folk that you speak o'.
Wir freens for mony lang years
An tae hear thir guid name bein tarnished
Brings me heartfelt sorrow an tears.

Thir's folk in that hoose that are worthy,
Done lots tae help oot in this toon
Nivir blate tae offer free service
An cash, whin the alms bowl comes roon.

If that lad hiz done wrang, as ye stated
Thir no ah tae be branded the same
Aye slip that wiz made by a youngster
Shouldna serve tae destroy thir guid name.

Noo's the time fir freens an guid neebors
Tae show whit guid spirit they bear
Wi a han' shak, an erm roon a shooder,
An a quiet wee word in an ear.

I'm hopin they'll say, "Jist ring me.
Ony thing that ye want, I will dae.
I've always felt pert o this family
An yir problem is my problem tae."

Go hame lassie, see tae yir femily.
If ye hear gossip, check that it's true
Fir the next bit o scandal thir spreadin
Could very weel be aboot you.

Redemption

Jane Townsley

"Jesus loves you," Constance whispered as she offered a tract
to a lean man in a business suit. He brushed past her almost
knocking her off balance. Constance swallowed hard. "Jesus
loves you," she whispered again to a young mother who was
negotiating a twin pushchair around the busy shoppers. Even
the babies ignored her.

Constance glanced at the rest of her church group dotted along
the street, several of whom were engaged in conversation with
shoppers. They seemed to be faring better. How she hated this!
But the Pastor had said it was her Christian duty. Jesus said,
"Go into all the world and preach the Good News."
Furthermore, it was a command, not a suggestion, the Pastor
had added sternly.

Constance, resigned to her fate, tried again. "Jesus loves you,"
she whimpered to a large woman in a stained dress and baggy
red cardigan and offered the tract.

"Maybe He loves you, darlin' but not me!" the woman replied,
laughing. However she stopped, took the leaflet and turning it
over in her hand, read out loud "Jesus died to save sinners, not
the righteous". "Sinners, eh?"

"Yes," Constance replied quickly. "If you truly repent of your
sins the Lord is quick to forgive and you can have eternal life."
She was sure she had missed a bit. No matter how many times
she rehearsed, she always stumbled over the words when it
really mattered. The woman stared at Constance thoughtfully.
Constance's face was growing redder as she desperately
scoured her mind for the next part of her speech. It all

sounded so easy when she practiced in the bathroom mirror. In her imagination, she had preached to thousands. Now she chewed her bottom lip nervously.

"Live forever, eh? Don't know if I'd want to, 'least not around here." The woman laughed again and the laugh spread over her face and seemed to travel down through her body, shaking her to her toes. Suddenly she became serious and asked, "Have you converted anybody yet?"

"Eh... no." Constance admitted. How she wished the Pastor was here or the others. Already she doubted herself. How could she answer questions? She hoped the woman wouldn't ask anything.

"You're trying too hard, love," the woman said, as if they were conspirators. "Those your friends? You keep glancing at them."

"Yes," Constance admitted. "We've been sent to evangelise this area. It seems the others are doing well."

"But you're not." The woman gave a friendly snort. "Tell you what love, you look half frozen. What d'you say we go to my flat for a cuppy? It's just across the road. You can tell them we got talking about Jesus, eh?"

Constance gazed at the woman. It was most unusual but what would Jesus do? Surely He would have accepted... friend of sinners and all that. But would the Pastor approve? She was supposed to be handing out tracts. He hadn't said anything about socializing. Before she could refuse, her companion grabbed her arm and led her across the street and through a doorway. They climbed up the narrow staircase and the woman opened a door into a small but comfortable flat.

"Lily's my name, love. Best we introduce ourselves properly, eh?" Lily filled the kettle.

"Constance," Constance replied. Lily motioned to her to sit at the small table.

"Sorry it's so small. Moved in a week ago – had to leave that man. I'll have to move again when he finds out where I am. Won't take him long, I expect."

"You've left your husband?" Constance was shocked. "That's not allow..."

"Don't give me that!" Lily interrupted. "Look here!" She pulled up the sleeve of her cardigan to reveal several large bruises, now yellowing. "And a lump here..." Lily pointed to the side of her head. "Knocked clean unconscious so I was. Don't tell me God wants me to stay and get worse. Maybe a lot worse." Lily poured the tea.

Constance thought hard. What would the Pastor say? She recalled his voice from the pulpit. "The Lord hates divorce. Hates it!"

"I... I don't know what the Lord would want you to do," Constance admitted.

"Well, he sure don't want me getting beaten up again, honey," Lily laughed. "So I figure I'm moving on."

Constance sipped her tea. "If your husband finds you, you mean."

"No ifs. He will. He's been asking around the local landlords. Just a matter of time now... days even."

"What will you do?"

"I told you, I'll move. That's if I'm still able."

Constance looked puzzled.

"Look honey, the last time I was unconscious for hours. Next time, he might kill me."

"Can't you go to the police?"

Lily raised an eyebrow.

"Women's Aid?"

"Nah, I'll be fine on my own," Lily replied. "Just got to keep moving. If I'm away long enough, he'll take up with someone else."

"But where will you go?"

Lily shrugged. "I'll find somewhere."

Constance frowned. "If you get another place around here, he'll find you again."

Lily laughed. "Yes. Trouble is, I got nowhere else to go. No family, no friends. They all scarpered years ago."

Suddenly Constance knew what to do. It came as an inspiration, a bold revelation from heaven itself.

"I could put you up for a while. Of course, you'd have to be a believer and accept Jesus into your heart and all the other stuff the Pastor says..."

"The Pastor?"

"At the church I attend."

"So you follow the Pastor?"

"Yes, he's God's anointed."

"Who says?"

"He does."

"I see." Lily looked thoughtful. "What would the Pastor say if he knew you were offering me a place to stay?"

Constance thought hard. She imagined the Pastor asking, "Constance, have you prayed about this? We have an outreach centre that helps these people. The Good Samaritan paid for a hotel room. He didn't invite his neighbour home. It's foolhardy and dangerous."

Constance chewed at her lip. What was she thinking of? She should leave right now. She gazed tearfully at her new friend.

Lily went on. "No need to tell me what the Pastor would say. I see it in your face, but one thing you could tell me..."

"Yes?"

"If He knew you were offering me a place to stay, what would Jesus say?"

It took a moment but only a moment. Constance laughed and the laughter sounded and felt like freedom.

"Pack your things," she said. "You're coming home with me."

Statue

Annie Johnstone

Man Child. 18 Years of age
And ready to be Alpha.
Brave, stupid thing as you
shuffle along in your
ill - fitting uniform
Your mother cried for weeks
everytime she glanced at your
picture on the mantle
And your pops sat solemn
and old in the corner
Your boots army issue and
black as coal crunch over
gravel
Your good friend Tommy shakes
In your delicate hands
Grey dust fills the air
and fear fills your
Psyche
You wish to be home again
Within the Womb again
And there he stands before you
A German boy of little more
than 16 years old.
Blond and Stormy blue
Angelic
Mauser wants to chat face to
Face. Shakes a little.
Fires twice. And ends what never
Really began
Many people fought valiantly
Boys became men

Men became murderers
Murderers became civilians
But you lay there, the dust
Settled upon your skin
A grotesque statue behind a pillar
The baby. Crumpled and forgotten
Yet you smile obscenely at
Two hearts broken
And a woman wishing she had bled

The Note

Jane Townsley

Jeannie cradled the cup of warm tea. She was thirsty, but Aunt Helen had forgotten the sugar and it tasted bitter. She felt guilty about minding… ungrateful even. She should drink it to please everyone, but every sip made her grimace. She hoped her aunt wouldn't notice. If her aunt asked, she would tell her, politely. You had to be careful how you worded things; you might upset someone. She should be in school but they hadn't let her go. She worried about a note. There had to be one – Mrs Andrews got angry if you didn't bring it. Usually she read Grandma's note on the way to school. It always started,

"Please excuse Jeannie for being absent …" and then explained. One time she was ill and proud to hand it over. But most days Mrs Andrews would scrutinise the note and purse her lips, then she would say "Take your seat, Jeannie."

Mrs Andrews knew a lot about Jeannie's Dad. Mrs Andrews knew a lot about everyone. Her husband was the minister and she went with him to visit people in trouble. Sometimes they came to the house and Jeannie was sent upstairs while they prayed in the living-room. Jeannie's mother had been killed in the crash and her father had been driving and blamed himself, even though the coroner's report said it was not his fault. The prayers went unanswered but they didn't stop. One night, Jeannie crept downstairs and overheard Mrs Andrews saying,

"It's not death that causes the pain, it's love. If you hadn't loved her, would it hurt so much?"

Aunt Helen patted her hand. "You have to talk, Jeannie. Tell me what's going on in here." Helen tapped her forehead.

I don't have to tell you anything, Jeannie thought, as a wave of anger surged. Yesterday she had overheard Uncle George telling Grandma that he would "try to talk" to her. Uncle George had never "tried" before. He either talked or he didn't. Everyone was acting weird, and if she knew what they wanted her to say, she would say it so they would leave her alone.

"You have to let the pain out," Aunt Helen continued, her voice uncharacteristically full of pity. "It's not healthy to hold it... Oh, I didn't mean... "

She wants me to cry, Jeannie thought. Then she'll stop fussing. But the tears wouldn't come. There was a heaviness, a numbness, a gaping hole where the pain should be. And there was anger – the kind of anger that she instinctively knew would projectile vomit over everyone if she dared let it escape. It was a rage that might never stop and there would be an awful mess to clear up afterwards. She didn't want to talk. She didn't want to listen. What she wanted... really wanted...

Jeannie put her cup on the table and stood up.
"Where are you going?" Aunt Helen seemed annoyed at the interruption. "Oh, all right."

The bathroom was at the end of the hallway, but the front door offered freedom.

Outside in the sunshine, she ran. She didn't take the town road past the school but the back path - towards the open countryside. Had she realised, she would not have gone this way because it was here, on the outskirts, that the cemetery lay. She was at the cemetery gates before she stopped, gasping for breath. She glanced behind to check she hadn't been followed.

Jeannie gripped the railings. She had wanted away from this horror and yet she had run towards it. Why? The place looked different today, almost welcoming. Maybe she could go inside.

The gates were open.

She avoided going directly to the grave, but she could not prevent her eyes from straying. The wreaths lay untouched from yesterday. From a distance they made a vibrant display, a rich splash of colour in an otherwise green grass and grey marble setting. Anyone could tell that this was a new grave, a fresh death. There was no headstone yet but she'd overheard them discussing it. The adults had chosen the words carefully, even asking her opinion. She had been watching TV and wouldn't be interrupted. Grandma had said that "loving son and father" was to be inscribed under his name, and did she think that was okay? In response, Jeannie had turned the volume up. She wondered what she was supposed to have said. "Oh yes, what a brilliant idea." Anyway, she thought now, loving son maybe, but loving father? She was sure that he did love her. But loving? Loving implies showing love. Loving dads don't hurt everyone by crying all the time. Loving dads don't do bad things to themselves and leave everyone else to sort the mess.

Some birds chirped. They didn't mind that this was a graveyard, a garden of death. She wandered around, whistling in communion with them. It was comforting to make sounds again. She couldn't remember the last time she had spoken out loud, certainly not since yesterday's funeral. She whistled louder.

Bravely, she drew nearer. A small voice inside her head encouraged her. Just another row. You can do it. A little closer. Two rows distance was enough. She sat down irreverently on a grave, leaning her frame against the headstone. Well done, the voice whispered. Enjoy the sound of the birds. She listened.

The chirping grew louder and apart from the occasional breeze rippling through the trees, there was peace. That was what Reverend Andrews had said to Grandma. "May he rest in peace." Maybe he does, but everyone else is in turmoil.
The warmth of the sun seemed to energise her, promising that the world would be alright again – that despite everything, life would continue. At least, for her.

Gathering courage, she rose and moved forward again. A few short steps and she was there. She wondered if it *was* an accident that she had taken this route. She could have cut across the field and walked by the river. Maybe she had intended to be here. No, needed to be….with him… one last time.

She stared at the flowers. Yesterday the masses of orange and yellow and purple contrasted sharply with the background of black. Black cars, black suits, black hats, black robes…

She stooped now to read the cards. "God bless…" "In Deepest sympathy…" "Love you forever.." "You will be sorely missed…"

One wreath at the centre spelled out "Dad". Someone else had chosen it. Someone else had written the card for her. A small fold of pink paper was tucked inside. Jeannie reached down and pulled it free. It said simply, "It's not death that causes the pain. It's love. From Mrs A."

Suddenly, loving didn't seem a wrong word. He had been loving and he had been loved. Precious memories of happier times surfaced, her mother and father laughing and joking. In fact, love seemed to be the only word that mattered now. She embraced the pain and began to cry.

Towing And Fro'ing

Janet McKenzie

The car engine coughed, spluttered and died as I exited the mini-roundabout and coasted to a stop, uncomfortably near the busy intersection . I glared at the petrol gauge, which was only just touching red. And I was on my way to the petrol station! It clearly wasn't my fault.

I put on my hazard flashers and reached for my mobile. Jack didn't sound exactly pleased to be summoned to my rescue.

"Could you get a can of petrol and meet me at the car?" I suggested. We lived less than half a mile away, so I expected him to be with me in under ten minutes. Then I'd pick up my friend and make for Perth.

Ten minutes passed….then fifteen. It was darkening now.

Passing drivers glared at the idiot parked so awkwardly near a corner.

When Jack finally arrived, drawing up in front of me, I shot out of the car and greeted him heatedly.

"What kept you? I've been waiting for ages!"

"Well, I was busy," he explained mildly. "You're lucky I bothered to answer the phone at all, but I thought it was Jock about the golf. And I'd quite a hunt for the tow-rope in the garage."

"The tow-rope?" I repeated in horror, only then noticing what dangled from his hand. "Where's the petrol?"

"You've got to have a special can nowadays to be legal. Much better just to tow you round to the petrol station."

Already he was fixing the rope linking the two cars.

"But I don't know how to be towed !" I protested.

"Just put it into neutral and let off the hand brake as I take up the slack. It's easy," he assured me, getting into his car.

"Oh God!" I said aloud, putting the car out of gear as he moved off slowly in front of me. The snake of tow-rope straightened and tightened as my car shuddered and moved. But it didn't move forward. It took off at a crazy angle to the right, aiming directly at a row of cars, parked end-on in a bay at the other side of Reform Street.

I wrestled with the steering-wheel, but it wouldn't budge. I stamped hard on the foot-brake which hit the floor with no effect on the speed of the car.

Everything went into slow motion. I could hear myself shouting as I prepared to write-off thousands of pounds worth of gleaming motor. I was aware of Jack stopping on my left, his outraged face watching in disbelief as I overtook him. I wrenched on the hand-brake, and my car came to a halt, inches from a Subaru Impreza.

Jack was at my window in seconds. No "Are you all right , Darling?" but "What the hell do you think you're doing? Don't tell me you didn't have your ignition on?"

"How was I supposed to know about the ignition?" I yelled back, enraged.

"Surely you know that if you don't have the ignition switched on, your steering's locked and your foot-brake doesn't work."

"How was I supposed to know all that? You never said a word about the blooming ignition!"

During this altercation we were blocking the road, one car on the left, another slewed across to the right, and a taut tow-rope knee-high between. Cars were tailed back to the corner.

Amazingly, nobody hooted or attacked us in a bout of road-rage. One driver helpfully controlled the traffic. We straightened ourselves out and put the show on the road again, this time with ignition on and steering and footbrake operational.

Somehow, we arrived at the petrol pumps with no damage done, except maybe to our reputations.

"Ken that wife McKenzie? Aye, used to teach up at the Hill. Shoutin at her man in Reform Street! Drunk? Coulda been....." Twenty pounds worth of petrol later, tow rope disconnected, Jack was set to go.

As I certainly wasn't speaking to him, I didn't suggest he waited.

Five minutes and ten attempts to start the car later, I regretted my pride. To my great embarrassment, I felt tears of frustration welling up. There was a knock on my car window. A young man, who looked familiar.

"Are you okay, Mrs McKenzie?"

"Not really. I ran out of petrol and now it won't start."

"Would you like me to have a go? Sometimes you need to boot it really hard."

And that's what he did, and it worked perfectly. The kindness of former pupils always amazes me. They must have very forgiving natures.

En route for Perth, I told my friend the story, ending with my plans for a quick divorce.

In the end I changed my mind. Husbands can be useful. You never know when you might need a tow.

A Way Of Looking

Janet McKenzie

I've no difficulty waking in the morning. It's sleeping that's problematic. I've never got used to the empty space beside me in bed. It's usually a relief when my phone chirps at 06:30 and another exciting day begins at my Bed and Breakfast.

My first thought is always about Moira. As time passes, images have become less painful. Sometimes there's even a happy memory of our time together, surprising me into a smile. I don't expect someone else to feature in my waking consciousness. It's happened a few times lately and it seems like some sort of betrayal.

I've a fair number of regulars at my B&B – mostly tradesmen who do contract work locally, or sales reps. Nowadays, Bellevue is hardly a home from home. Since Moira went three years ago, I've let standards drop and things become a bit basic, but it's clean, the breakfast is adequate and I set my prices accordingly. So, when a Mrs Carmichael calls to book a room for one night, I nearly turn her down. She doesn't sound at all like the type of person who'd be happy at Bellevue.

"It's for myself and my elderly mother," she says. "We must have the room on the first floor, with the bay window facing the sea."

I begin to explain the situation.

"Mr Allan, I've checked things out," she interrupts. "I know Bellevue has changed. But my mother is extremely keen to visit there again, while she's still able to get about. She has such powerful memories of the house, from her young days. Please indulge her."

Several times, before the ladies are due to arrive, I feel sorry I agreed. When Moira and I rescued and refurbished the house, it still bore signs of a rather grand past – oak panelling and plaster cornices - dating from long before. I feel sure the old lady'll be disappointed to see it now and I'm surprised that this worries me.

The ladies arrive in a well-kept green Rover, and Mrs Carmichael parks near the front door. I go out to carry their overnight bags. I don't usually offer such courtesies, but Mrs Carmichael looks to be around seventy, and her mother, Mrs Kerr, is very elderly indeed. She grips her daughter's arm firmly and walks with a straight back.

"You know there's no lift?" I ask.

Mrs Carmichael nods. "We'll manage very well. We're used to stairs, aren't we, Mother?"

"Certainly! Stairs are excellent for the circulation!"

As they enter Bellevue, Mrs Kerr turns her head, moving her gaze round the hall. "Lovely," she says. "Just as I remember it."

I've a quick look around, but all I notice is scuffed woodwork and dingy wallpaper. I feel ashamed. What would Moira think of Bellevue now? I go in front of them with the bags, pushing open the door to the stairs with my shoulder.

"This is new," remarks Mrs Kerr ."There was never a door here."

"Fire regulations," I explain and she nods, satisfied.

As I lead the way upstairs, I wonder what they'll think of their room. These considerations don't normally bother me but I don't want this old woman to be too disappointed.

She manages the stair well - they only once pause for breath - and stops on the landing. "I'm so looking forward to seeing the view!" she enthuses.

This is bad! I lay down the cases and turn to her daughter.

There's been a horrible misunderstanding. But Mrs Carmichael shakes her head and presses her lips together. I shrug and open the door, standing back to let mother and daughter enter the room.

Sunlight, flooding in, crudely highlights the worn furnishings and the faded carpet, once Moira's favourite shade of blue. Mrs Kerr frees her arm and takes several steps forward, into the large bay window.

"Look, Margaret!" she cries. "The view! Isn't it fine?"

Mrs Carmichael moves beside her. "Lovely, Mother," she agrees quietly.

"Are there boats in the harbour? I can't quite make out."

"Yes. Several fishing boats and lots of small boats."

"Pleasure boats." Mrs Carmichael nods. "Good. And no warships in the bay?"

"No, Mother."

"Thank God. No warships these days."

I start to inch my way towards the door. Things are getting out of hand. These two normal-looking women are seriously bonkers. Mrs Kerr must sense my feelings. She turns in my direction but her eyes seem to focus just beyond my head.

Now I understand.

"Mr Allan, I should explain. When I used to come here, the bay was full of warships – destroyers, battleships, frigates."

"During World War Two," I say, relieved. "I've heard about that."

"It was a dreadful time but for me there were some blissful days among the dark ones. My husband and I were newly married. We were really too young and our parents were against it at first but Harry was in the navy and when war was declared, marriage seemed the only thing to do."

She turns her eyes towards the window again.

"He was stationed here for three months. Whenever he got shore leave, I came to Bellevue to be with him." She pauses. "When he finally sailed for active service, he asked me to stand in this window and wave. Then he could see me from the ship's deck. I couldn't see him amongst the others but I waved and waved until the ship was round the headland and out of sight."

For the first time, her voice becomes unsteady. "Harry never came back. His ship was lost, with all the crew."

I don't know what to say, so I look out of the window instead. Not that there's much to see, since they built the retirement complex bang in front of us. Just after Moira died and I'm glad she never saw it. Bellevue. Silly name now.

I mutter something about letting them settle in, tell them about local restaurants for dinner and make my escape.

Later, after I've heated and eaten a lasagne from the freezer, I wander into the back garden. It's had years of neglect - for a long time I couldn't go there - but somehow it's still full of vigour, producing colour every season from plants and shrubs whose names I can never remember.

Moira learned the names. She loved the garden, although she'd never had one before we came to Bellevue.

"A real gardener lived here," she'd say as each month presented some fresh delight, from the drifts of spring flowers to the fiery foliage of a winter shrub. "Maybe they totally neglected the house, but the garden shows real TLC!"

For sure, the house had been neglected - much of it virtually abandoned. That's the only reason we could afford it.

I walk slowly along the paths, overgrown in places by grass and weeds, and reach Moira's favourite rose. I stop to breathe its scent, and immediately I'm reminded of Moira's last Christmas.

Along with dozens of other men, I'd wandered into a large store's perfume department, hoping for inspiration - and amazingly it came to me, wafting from a nearby counter, transporting me back to a summer afternoon.

"This is our new fragrance," an advisor was telling another clueless customer. "What does it suggest to you?"
"Roses!" I interrupted. "Not just any rose, either. My wife's favourite rose!"

I stand now with my eyes closed, reliving that Christmas morning. I was nervous. Had I got it right? Could I really identify a scent of summer in December? Would she recognise it?

She did! "Rosa Odorata Pallida!" she breathed. "Oh, you clever, clever darling!"

I'm smiling now, remembering. I walk on, enjoying the warmth, still there in the evening sun. From the house next door comes a muffled beat. Val's son, practising with his mates. They've rock band ambitions. Val is my new neighbour. Last week, she called to me across the wall, asking if I fancied a beer. I surprised myself by going round to her garden and staying for more than an hour, just chatting like I haven't done for ages. Nothing too personal but I felt relaxed with her. Now, I look over the wall, half hoping she'll be at her kitchen window but there's no sign of her. I'm disappointed. Then, as I walk into the house, I feel guilty. How can I be thinking about Val so soon after remembering Moira?

Next morning, I'm up earlier than usual, preparing to make a real effort over breakfast. Three of my regulars from a local building site are complimentary about my Full English Breakfast but the ladies later opt for scrambled eggs - a speciality of mine.

"No-one can make them like you," Moira used to say. "Creamy and succulent."

They go down well. I feel unfamiliarly pleased. I carry their bags to the car and then pour Mrs Kerr a last cup of tea while her daughter checks their room.

"Margaret's so good, taking time to come here with me, in spite of all her other interests and commitments," says Mrs Kerr when we're alone. "And it was Margaret who kept me going, when I might have felt my life was over. A baby's a great reason to get on with it."

She takes a sip of tea and replaces the cup carefully on the saucer. "You're a widower?" she asks.

I find myself telling her about Moira - how we'd been soul-mates, meeting in foster care as teenagers and knowing from the start that we belonged together, how the small amounts of family money we'd inherited had been pooled to buy a mobile burger bar and how we'd worked our socks off to expand and make our business successful enough to sell out and buy the run-down Bellevue. But how, with Moira having died, it all seems a bit pointless.

I finish my story and feel a bit disappointed when she immediately turns the conversation back to herself.

"I loved Harry dearly," she tells me, "and I had our little daughter to care for. Perhaps it could have been enough. But my life has been wider than that. After a while, a new husband, two sons, and an interesting job. Later, grandchildren, great grandchildren and a host of interests."

She pauses to drink her tea. Bully for you! I think.

"But you, Mr Allan!" she announces forcibly, almost banging down her cup. "You've rather let things go, haven't you? Given up on life? Just coasting along?"

Her tone is withering, her not-quite-on-target gaze disconcerting.

"Yet you're still a young man, with much more to contribute to the world. It's a tragic mistake, you know, when one life ends, to let two lives be finished."

I'm speechless - and furious. What right has this ancient crone to lecture me?

"I see a lot more than Margaret realises," she adds quietly as her daughter approaches, "but the best pictures are in my head."

When she's settled her mother in the car, Margaret comes round to where I'm standing and shakes my hand. "Thank you," she says. "Thank you for not spoiling her memories. They're very precious to her."

I nod, wish them a safe journey, wave them off and stand for a while looking after the car, my anger cooled. I have precious memories too, like Mrs Kerr, and vibrant pictures in my head. The difference is, she hasn't let them smother her energy or kill her emotions. She's got more oomph in her at ninety-plus than I've got at fifty!

I turn and walk inside, knowing I've reached a turning point. I was getting there by myself, slowly, but the old lady has fairly spun me round.

Suddenly I'm dizzy, with a new, beautiful view of the future.

Echo Dust

Annie Johnstone

Her voice is in the cupboard
Would you like to hear it clearer?
Stroke, soothe, calm and caress
Pinch, grab, clamp in duress

Her mind is in the basement you
Could ask her now and again. Word.
Hits home it shakes and spatters. Esteem
Shatters, in shards it scatters

Her heart is in the ice box along
With your refreshments for the game
She imagines walking, he glares mocking
No talking, pride blocking

Her soul is in an elevator
The button stuck on down
With the blues and black she won't
Be back eyes closed she hits the ground

Trespass

Annie Johnstone

Careful little wildflower. That one is not like the others
He came tumbling down the hill not because he fell
But because he was pushed and the perpetrator poured
Salt in the wounds at the bottom

He had tried for the part of woodcutter but was branded
The wolf and in a rage of blackest night he fled
To the deepest, darkest part of the forest
There he built himself a castle made of sticks and stones

This palatial purgatory became a fortress, fortified
To defend against attacking golden locks with fireflies
The walls made of steel to prevent passions whilst
The roof repelled all chances

But you are a master thief, honey bunch, disguised
As sunset and by extreme intelligence and dry
Wit you broke in and stole what had blackened,
Burned and wept for unjust love affairs

You did it for fun and challenge, my dear, but what
You hold if not kept safe and sated
Will fizzle in your hands like bitter sherbet.
It will turn to the rankest of poisons

And it will finish what you so foolishly started.

A Berryfield Bonus

Jessie Nellies

It's mony years noo, at the time o' the Fair
When Ah ran intae wee Paisley Terry.
"Ah'm fed up an' broke," he said in despair.
"Let's run up tae Blair tae the berries."

Weel, we walked till we'd blisters an' cadged a few lifts,
We were weet, we were cauld an' fair hungry,
But still we got here, eftir lang weary oors
On the back o' an auld coalman's lorry.

We steyed in a hut alang at the braes,
Eck Petrie took peety upon us,
Sayin' "Pick ev'ry day as lang as it's fine
An' ye'll share in the berryfield bonus".

On the Setterday nicht we haud up tae the hall,
Wi' the money we'd made at the pickin'.
We were dusted an' polished an' thocht we looked fine,
Weel, we micht get a click at the jiggin'.

There by the stage stood this big busty blonde,
Here goes, Ah'll ask her tae dance.
She said, "Sorry, wee man, ye're jist no ma type,
But there's wan fella in wi' a chance.

Jist look ower there at that snappy grey suit.
They tell me he's got a big car,
An if Ah hae ma wey, he'll be takin' me oot.
Wi' his sort Ah feel Ah'll go far."

So Ah settled for Meg, we'd met at the job,
A nice lass an' really quite bonnie.
We winched for twa weeks, then Ah hid tae haud hame,
Aye, back tae the wark an' the worry.

We wrote back and forrit an' met when we could,
In thae days there wisna the cash,
An' eftir a spell we decided tae wed,
For Ah worshipped my berryfield lass.

Weel, times werena easy, wi' twa growin' bairns,
But we'd come back tae Blair noo an' then,
But then they grew up, nae short runs for them,
They'd jist jump on a jet oot tae Spain.

Then the missus an' me thocht we'd hae a run up
An' see fowk we kent in the toon,
Jist wander aboot, hae a look an' a chat,
An' jist hae a guid nosey roon.

We were in Leslie Street when the wife poked ma ribs,
She said, "Look, there's the girl o' yir dreams,
There's that big brozey wumman wi' lang stringy hair,
An' grease poorin' oot at the seams".

Weel, a' Ah could dae, wis tae look mystified,
Ah jist couldna think whit she'd mean,
Bit Ah kent there wis mischief ahint her remark,
By the wicked wee glint in her een.

"Aye, that wis yir dream girl, she got her dream man,
An' pair thing, she's hert sorry noo,
For the suit wisna his, nae mair wis the car,
He jist drove it for Colonel McKew.

"Oh," I sighed in relief, wiped the sweat fae ma broo
Whin Ah thocht whit ma fate could hae been,
Then Ah fell back on the plea alud men yaise,
"Och, ye've no muckle sense at nineteen."

Noo Ah'll coont ma blessins Ah got the richt lass,
We're lucky, no much comin' ower us,
Ah'm content wi' ma Meg for nigh forty year,
Aye, she wis ma berryfield bonus!

Ericht Catches

Catriona Ward Sell

first sounds of this new place:
waves breaking backwards on weir,
water under bridge where
salmon leap, not arched like dolphins
but splashing straight as sticks
      collies chase

I've crashlanded in Rattray
in my parents' new house
with our old things;
      a comfort space which has changed shape.
My makeshift loft bedroom, unfamiliar
holds my childhood bed
and the river-rush song drives through the ajar window,
lulling

I don't know if my return is an escape
or a knowing when to give up;
      when to stop chasing storms elsewhere
          when to accept,
          when to return

but my storm still rages in mind.
and although the river soothes,
the salmon invite:

sometimes, I want to swim;
sometimes, to leap -

      and sometimes, to be caught

Life Line

Barbara Lynch

I yearn for you when being apart,
your ruggedness I crave
I need to walk your lowland ways
and breathe your crystal air
The sun, the wind, the sparkling sea
are in my mind, my soul
Apart from you I'm incomplete
I need you more and more
My life line, my Scotland

Mayfield Hall

Elizabeth Leslie

Last year I drove along Arbroath Road in Dundee looking for
Mayfield Hall. To my disappointment my old student hostel
has been demolished, and smart new houses now stand in its
place! However, I still have my memories....

In October 1963, fresh out of Perth High School and eager to
start my teacher training course at Dundee College of
Education, I arrived at Mayfield. The huge Victorian building
was buzzing with excitement that Monday afternoon as scores
of young women settled in, and by five-thirty pm we were all
gathered for our evening meal in the enormous dining room,
part of the new modern extension. There Miss Bicket, the
statuesque, middle-aged warden welcomed us before very
firmly spelling out the rules.

The dining room consisted of long tables holding twelve girls
each. At our weekday evening meals we had our assigned
seats, which we occupied for the entire year. We all had to be
in our places before Miss Bicket entered, accompanied by her
'guests', two different students each day. While they had table
service, it was strictly controlled self-service for everyone else,
with one table at a time allowed to the serving hatch where we
were dished up hearty platefuls of nourishing food.

A strident bell summoned us to each meal. It also woke us
every morning, at 7am on weekdays, slightly later at
weekends, with the breakfast bell half an hour later. Breakfast
held none of the formality of the evening meal though; we
could sit where we liked and there was no sign of the warden.

Being a female-only establishment, there were strict rules about male friends. They were permitted in the entrance hall or common rooms only. On no account were they allowed upstairs! Being caught with a boyfriend in your bedroom would have meant instant dismissal from Mayfield, and possible expulsion from College as well.

Boyfriends however *were* welcomed to the official parties held once a year. My first year party in June 1964 was a grand affair for which we all dressed up. Complete with buffet and a live band, it was held in the main common room, suitably decorated for the occasion.

This room also became the focus of much excitement in January 1964. For the first time, Mayfield Hall was to have a television! This proved to be a popular move, and the first Thursday evening after its arrival we all crowded in to watch 'Top of the Pops' where The Beatles were the star attraction. Thereafter, each Thursday saw the common room packed by 7.30 pm, with the early arrivals filling up the chairs and sofas and floor at the front, while the latecomers made do with standing at the back.

Of course life in Mayfield had its serious side too. Apart from the regular course work, there were the twice yearly exams to prepare for. During exam week there would be a quieter atmosphere in the building. Some students liked to revise together; I preferred to study alone in my room, emerging occasionally to make yet another cup of coffee in the little kitchen along the corridor.

Then there was teaching practice, during which time we would spend our evenings preparing lessons and teaching aids for the next day. The night before a 'crit' lesson (when one of our college tutors would observe us) was particularly important. Everything had to be right – our final grades depended on this. And sometimes there was the unpleasant and the unexpected!

During my second year a bad bout of flu confined me to bed for four days. It seemed eerily silent while everyone else was out at College, the only indications that I wasn't completely alone in the building being Miss Bicket's daily visit to take my temperature and a maid bringing my lunch on a tray. Ill though I was, it a relief to hear the noise and chatter of the girls returning late in the afternoon.

After two years in Mayfield, my three friends and I decided to 'live out' in our third year, and moved into a rented house in Thompson Street, off Perth Road. And while I enjoyed my year of independence I will always remember Mayfield with affection – the fun, the friendships, and above all that strict but reassuring presence – the warden!

(First published in 'Scottish Memories')

Reekie Linn

Dawn Mullady

I know this is my favourite place
He accepts me into his beautiful space
No critiques, no judgements, just who I am
No need for stress as he is so calm

My favourite place I can take you there
Clues in this poem are written with flair
Follow the words you may find it too
Keep this a secret between me and you

My favourite place with rivers and falls
You'll quietly hear the birds and their calls
Open, open, open your eyes
See snow on the hills and sun in the skies

My favourite place just walk to the path
Breathe in the air releasing your wrath
Step by step you'll pass the falls
Keep to the left see the best of all

My favourite place he's quite a height
Descend his slopes with all your might
Get off the track not quite there yet
Wild terrain you'll get stuck I bet

My favourite place he's dangerous too
Be very careful when admiring his views
Ten mins from the path you're nearly there
It gets quite tough so please beware

My favourite place he`s worth the risk
Touching his heart I could never miss
His heart flows with so much style
So beautiful you`ll stay a while

My favourite place is not just mine
I share his space from time to time
Not made of concrete, metal or tin
So natural, he is my Reekie Linn

My favourite place it's time to go
Up the slopes where his waters flow
The Isla Glen is where he is hidden.
You will return as you`ll be smitten.

Shadows: A Sestina

Catriona Ward Sell

After we have climbed this sunlit mountain
we'll turn to see our shadows on the water
feeling the blaze of the sun at our back,
with outstretched arms, blocking the light,
silhouetting our flying selves below, a mark
on a loch otherwise as blue as sky.

And as we cast our cares into the sky
we'll believe that we could move this mountain,
as we set ourselves the highest mark:
to fly over the seas, and cross the waters,
to travel, and to love, and see the light
never doubt again, never looking back.

But when we descend from that high, turn back
towards our roots, forget we touched the sky,
we'll realise our shadows are not so light
to carry forwards, with pressure mounting
to follow footsteps with ease of treading water –
shadows of expectation: an ancestral mark.

Because shadows are rucksacks, they mark
our shoulders and arms, cut into our backs:
we need them, they're our supplies and water
and guide us under this unforgiving sky,
yet we need them not, heavy as mountains,
obscuring the view, and blocking out the light.

This expectation weights us, stops our flight;
in time, we'll forget these desires to mark
out our own skies, or climb our own mountains,
preoccupied with thoughts of looking back
for how those before us regarded the sky:
sheltering from its sun, cursing its water.

Or we will realise, in time, what a
hard dream it is to fly, when dreams of flight
are held close by all, and clutter the sky,
and we'll wonder: will this be our only mark?
Will our own trace of flight, when we look back
be when our shadows fell on lone mountains?

But for now, this mountain's ours, and the water
reflects back our flying shadows against blue light
and we will set our mark by it: the limit is the sky.

National Trust

Catriona Ward Sell

Eight centuries of footsteps echo
through rooms which get smaller
as my key turns. The must of sadness
follows down spiral staircases,
hides behind portcullises,
defines this place

I re-arrange the furniture,
check off inventories.
prepare the ghost stories of tomorrow

in fact: the lords of Kellie
kept a garden, liked architecture
fought at Culloden
but tourists prefer to trust
in murders behind battlements
and blood stained carpets

and as I flick the final light
I see a shadow flinch
to hide behind an empty cradle.
        quick as a bat -
        silent as a pulse

I pounce. A murdered child
trapped in a cradle; a Jacobite prince
suffocated in sleep – tomorrow,
my story shivers foreign spines,
sells tartan
        (somewhere in the past
        a child killed in a civil war

has known no such romance)

and I wonder what happens
when I cycle downlane.
If the ghosts, caught between
the glossary and the gossip
are heard walking the short corridor
between history and veneer;
trapped between cruel fact
and thin brochures

Yes, this is a claustrophobic country.
Our lies push us in,
fatten us with ghostpride,

help to bury us

The Berries

Elizabeth Leslie

Driving around Perthshire, the sight of raspberry fields always takes me back to my fifties childhood when, along with my Mum and two sisters, I spent each summer holiday 'at the berries'. For despite the early starts and the hard work I loved the exciting new dimension it brought to my life.

The first treat of the day was boarding the 'berry bus', a white double-decker belonging to McLennans of Spittalfield. Full of noisy, excited children and their long-suffering mums, it drove us some six miles to the berry farm near Bankfoot. Once on board, the older children and teenagers rushed upstairs, while the mums stayed downstairs with the smaller children. And while the mums gossiped, the children sang, old favourites like 'Ten Green Bottles' and 'The Quartermaster's Store' and whatever else was popular at the time.

On arrival we piled out of the bus and into the berry field, where the gaffer assigned a 'dreel' to each pair of pickers. And after hanging our coats on the end post, tucking our piece bags in the bushes, and collecting our berry pails from the huge pile at the top of the field, we were ready to start.

One on either side of the bushes, we carried our pails to the far end of the dreel, doing our best to avoid a nasty scratch from a protruding stray branch. And after a rainy night we would try to dodge the wet bushes that slapped against us as we squelched down the muddy dreel in our wellies.

My younger sister and I were too small to reach the higher branches at first. So Mum and my older sister took a side each, while we were their helpers, picking the lower berries. After a few years, however, we had grown tall enough to stretch to the top berries, and were allowed our own sides.

Once our big pails were full, we took them to 'the weights'. Stationed at the top of the field was a flat cart on which were huge hanging scales, a row of barrels and table with a money box. We would heave the pail up to the weights man who deftly emptied the berries into the weighing pail then hung it on the scales, noting the weight before tipping the berries into one of the barrels.

Then came the exciting bit. We were paid there and then, according to how much we had picked. When we started in the early fifties the rate was a penny ha'penny per pound of berries, so picking eight pounds of rasps would earn us a shilling. Proudly tucking our earnings into the little drawstring purses attached to our belts, we would return to our dreel, eager to make some more. And after several such trips in a day, counting up our money at night was a satisfying business. Of course, it wasn't non-stop work! We had a morning break at 10 o'clock and a longer stop around noon. During these 'picnics' we would gather at the top of our dreel, where Mum would hand round egg or cheese sandwiches and big slices of home-made fruit loaf, all washed down with orange squash or tea from the flask. Then it was back down the dreel to start work again.

By half past four we were beginning to wilt, and the shout 'There's the berry bus' would be met with cheers of relief. Emerging from our dreels, we would hurry to the weights for the last time, before heading for the bus.

Over tea, we would recount the day's adventures to our Dad. Then it would be a wash and an early night, while Mum prepared clothes and food for the next day, then took a well-earned breather.

Meanwhile, our money boxes were filling up, and when the berries were over there would be a shopping trip to Perth or Dundee, where we could spend our berry money on something special. I bought my first watch one year. Another year it was a tennis racquet.

Then it was time to return to school, and in the excitement of being in a new class with a new teacher, berry time was soon forgotten – until the next summer when the magic started all over again!

(First published in 'Scottish Memories')

The Last Straw

Barbara Lynch

It was the summer of 1958 and at 16 years old I was to be presented to the Queen at Lauriston Castle Edinburgh.

Why was I chosen? Her Majesty and the Duke of Edinburgh were to meet with representatives from The Association of Mixed Clubs and Girls Clubs in Scotland. Our Girls Club was the smallest and we were requested to send one member. At our weekly Club meeting all our names were put into a hat and my name was drawn. I can still remember the butterflies in my tummy at that moment. They would visit me a few times in the lead up to the "Big Day".

After the initial letter, a gold embossed invitation in my name arrived and we decided that our leader, Miss Gardiner, would accompany me. I was so nervous but she assured me that all would be well! What was I to wear? Obviously something special and so Mum, Miss Gardiner and I went on a shopping spree to various towns in the surrounding area.

On the list were a posh dress, hat, gloves, shoes and bag. With two months to go, everyone thought there was lots of time to find what I needed. The dress was found and I loved it. It was pale blue with a floral design and had a beautiful pale blue sash. The smaller items followed in due course. However the hat proved much more difficult.

Our yearly Club outing was due and that year we were going to Broughty Ferry beach near Dundee. So, in another attempt to buy the illusive hat, my Mother and I were dropped off in Dundee with the promise that we could join the group later.

We searched in a few shops before we finally found a straw boater-style hat with blue ribbon. It looked grand and was just the thing to set off my outfit. Thank goodness the problem was solved because I was desperate to join my friends swimming in the sea and the picnic that would follow. The sun was shining and, with the outfit complete, all seemed perfect.

To reach the others as quickly as possible we took a taxi, a rare treat. We arrived and I could see the others laughing and having fun in the sea. Moments later I was changed into my swimsuit and running down the beach toward waiting friends and glistening waves. Suddenly, down I went, crashing into a hole in the sand, and a dreadful pain shot up my right leg. I remember screaming in agony and the next thing I was aware of was being surrounded by a sea of very anxious faces, most of course I recognised. Mum was there holding my hand and trying to reassure me, saying that someone had gone to get a doctor and that I mustn't move. Why hadn't I noticed the sand castles and nearby hole in the sand?

Soon a Doctor appeared and bent down to examine my very swollen ankle. Tears ran down my face, the pain was hardly bearable and I was so afraid. Everyone looked worried for me. It was to have been such a happy day and here was I, spoiling it for everyone. I heard the doctor say that an ambulance would take me to hospital in Dundee. The ambulance crew arrived in no time at all and I was carefully lifted onto a stretcher and carried to the waiting vehicle.

The next while all seemed a blur, but some time later the good news was that my ankle wasn't broken but that I had torn the ligaments badly. The damaged area was soon strapped and bandaged and I was given instructions that I had to rest with my leg up until told otherwise. The question uppermost in our minds was would my ankle heal sufficiently during the next few weeks to enable me to stand long enough for my presentation to the Queen?

Thank goodness I had been practicing my bow and curtsey for weeks so now I rested and hoped that the healing process would begin. The District Nurse came to see me every few days. She admired my outfit, but would I ever get to wear it?

That straw hat had a lot to answer for as shopping for it had started off the disastrous event. However, it was wonderful news when I was given the go-ahead to practise walking again. During this time I had to read and remember the strict protocol when meeting the Queen. As I was presented, I had to say "Your Majesty" and then when answering any other questions put by the Queen I had to end my answer by adding "Mam".

A week before the big day our local GP visited and agreed that as long as I could sit before and after my presentation I could join the other Club members for our big day at the Garden Party, "Hooray"

My ankle would still be strapped but with a smaller bandage.

The Local newspaper carried the story with the Headline "Royal Day For Local Teenager" and I hoped it would all go without a hitch.

The big day arrived - I was so excited. Miss Gardiner and I joined the special coach in Perth for the journey to Edinburgh. With our glad rags on and photos taken, off we set.

Later, at Lauriston Castle, as I stood in the line to be presented, I could see Her Majesty making her way towards us. She looked so beautiful and perfectly dressed. She was accompanied by a representative from the Association of Clubs, who introduced us one by one. It all seemed a dream and yes, I did remember the correct way to address Queen Elizabeth. In that moment, I was no longer aware of my tightly strapped ankle as I made my curtsey and bowed my head.

To think that I nearly didn't make it because searching for that hat nearly was the "last straw" - it was a real straw hat after all and complemented my outfit just perfectly on the day I met the Queen.

The Village Dance

Elizabeth Leslie

Who can forget 1962 – the year of the Cuban missile crisis, Telstar and 'Love Me Do' by The Beatles?

But I remember 1962 for another reason. I was sixteen and going to my first dance. I'd been to the usual school parties before, but this was different – a real dance with a live band in our village hall!

Getting ready was all part of the fun and after I'd donned my full-skirted flowery dress, new nylons and high heels, I styled my hair into the latest Dusty Springfield bouffant. A layer of mascara, a touch of lipstick, a quick spray of Coty L'aimant and I was ready to go!

The three-piece Scottish dance band was warming up on stage as my friends and I crowded into the hall. Making for the girls' side, a riot of excited voices and coloured dresses, we sat down and surveyed the scene. The boys, most of whom we already knew, were hunched in groups on the opposite side of the hall, resplendent in suits and ties. While the shy ones squinted self-consciously over at us, their more confident counterparts openly surveyed us with much nudging and nodding.

A drum-roll announced the arrival of the MC, who strode across the stage, welcomed us all and announced the first dance, the Gay Gordons. Immediately there was swarm of boys across the floor, each eager to 'ask up' a girl. Soon we were all on the floor, marching and skipping our way round to the strains of 'The Bonnie Lass o' Bonaccord', with my partner, more at home on the farm than the dance floor, thudding out the steps with more energy than skill.

Dance followed dance – The Dashing White Sergeant, a St Bernard's Waltz, a quickstep, an Eightsome Reel – all dances we'd learned at school in preparation for our Christmas parties.

The most challenging of all was Strip the Willow. Here some of the boys became so exuberant as they swung their partners that one girl landed on the floor in a flurry of net petticoats.

Then came a great favourite- a Paul Jones. Everyone flooded onto the floor where the girls formed an inner circle, and the boys an outer one. When the band started playing, the circles walked round in opposite directions. Suddenly the music stopped and I was facing my next partner – the local dreamboat, complete with Elvis quiff and highly polished winkle-pickers! Aware of the envious glances and one or two glares from the other girls I waltzed off in his arms to the strains of 'Westering Home'. When this short dance ended, we re-formed our circles and went through the whole procedure again. This was repeated several times, each time resulting in a different, if less exciting, partner.

The excitement peeked when the Twist was announced. The floor filled up and soon we were all twisting to Chubby Checker's 'Let's Twist Again.' 'Round and round and up and down…' the song went, with some of the boys getting so carried away they ended up in a heap on the floor.

All too soon, it seemed, the last dance was announced. Traditionally, whoever asked you for the last dance walked you home. I waited with baited breath to see who it would be. And no – it wasn't one of the 'cool' older guys with the confident swaggers. It was the nice boy next door whom I'd known since I was two years old.

And later, while answering my younger sister's barrage of questions about my evening, there was only one question in my mind, 'When is the next dance?'

(First published in 'Scottish Memories')

Through The Chair

Alan Adair

As the large mahogany framed wall clock, with its richly toned chime, announced 10.00 am, the Chairman, the avuncular and rather tubby John Duncan, addressed the Committee.

"Gentlemen, I now call to order the 374th meeting of Blairgowrie Council."

As John Duncan looked around the large oval table, he was pleased to see that every member was present - bar one absentee who had made his excuse in writing.

He continued. "Our Secretary has received an apology from Angus Dunn who has another bout of consumption. But I am pleased to see that we have a dozen or so hale and hearty members, all ready tae address the issues of our day. Oh, and I'll introduce Charlie Robertson who has come to help Mr McGregor. So, withoot further ado - you will have all read the Minutes of the last meeting."

He pointed towards a blackboard behind him. On the board was chalked the agenda for that day's meeting. After "Apologies for Absence", the next item was "Minutes of the Council Meeting, 23rd March 1860."

Jimmy McGregor, who sat at one rounded end of the oak table, rasped a cough and waved a hand to catch the Chairman's attention. "I would like Mr Cuthbertson to expand on his statement in Minute 253.1"

"It's clear enough," retorted a smartly suited gentleman from the opposite end of the table.

The Chairman interjected. "Members please seek permission of the Chair before speaking. Or we risk wasting valuable time." In a pointed aside to a thin, pale skinned young gent on his left, "Read that Minute, Jim."

Jim obliged. "Minute 253.1 'Mr Cuthbertson proposed that anyone found in unauthorised possession of river trout should be summarily dealt with and drummed out.'"

"There you have it, from the Secretary," the Chairman continued. "There was no Seconder for that proposal but that brings us onto the next item - poaching on private lands."

To the chairman's right, two committee members were having a whispered exchange. One said, "Did you hear wee Jimmy McGregor caught Cuthbertson red-handed with a big catch o' brown trout?" The other replied, "Aye, but word is that 'Cuthy' has threatened to pull the rug on Jimmy's loans if he breathes a word."

"Gentlemen!" the Chairman roared at the two members and then went on, "Will you no stop behavin' like a pair o old fishwives and say what you have to through the *Chair*. Then perhaps we can all hear and join in!"

There followed a debate on poaching of fish and game. A common theme was that most of the culprits lived across the river in Rattray, therefore beyond the jurisdiction of the good people of Blairgowrie. One member suggested that the best deals on fresh salmon were from the shoemakers in Rattray. How else could one explain the abundance of fine footwear on children living that side of the river?

Another retorted that Blairgowrie should encourage more shoemakers and cobblers to establish businesses so folks wouldn't be embarrassed to see so many barefooted waifs in the town centre. It was pointed out that few shoemakers could afford the rents demanded by the town's landlords - rents that had led to an abundance of wine and spirit merchants: traders who could most readily pass on costs to willing customers. When someone opined that the bulk of those customers came from Rattray, it was generally agreed that there lay financial justice.

There was little the Blairgowrie Council could do about the poaching, other than assure everyone that all culprits would feel the full force of the law. It was agreed that posters be placed in prominent points in town and space taken in the local press to advertise the severity of punishment for any transgressor.

"We move onto the next item, the 'Status Report on Blairgowrie's Wells and Pumps'", said John Duncan, who added, "You know how important it is that we have a good supply of water. The proposed mains supply from the Lornty will promote improved health but is of foremost importance in supporting the financial well-being of our hotels and other businesses, who seek to benefit from the burgeoning tourist trade."

The Chairman continued, "As part of the viability study for the mains supply, Mr McGregor was asked to survey and report on our existing water supply. Over to you, Jimmy."

Jimmy McGregor coughed deeply and patted his chest three times so that nobody would think other than he was suffering from a severe affliction. He apologised for having a fearsomely sore throat and delivered by the syllable, "Sadly, we were unable to examine every well and pump in town, due to many being located on closed premises. However, we visited six hundred or so." He confessed, "I'm sorry about my throat. Charlie was going to cover the facts and figures but I think it better if he delivers the full report."

At this, Mr Cuthbertson became agitated and said, "Through the Chair, Mr Chairman. The member responsible for the report should deliver that report."

"Normally, Mr Cuthbertson," replied the Chairman.

"However, Mr McGregor is struggling with his throat and it would be a great relief, to him and this committee, if he were to pass the baton to Charlie."

Charlie Robertson, Jimmy's assistant, began to read. The report gave the status of the myriad of wells and pumps that he and Jimmy had visited. Most had deteriorated over the years. Pumps, some of which lacked basic maintenance, had replaced many wells. There were many on private properties, which he and Jimmy had been unable to visit. There were dozens of wells in basements of business establishments, but due to neglect, some proprietors depended on the nearest pump for their supply. Some wells were drawing from the same water source: an overdraw from one would restrict supply to both, with ensuing acrimony. Some linings had collapsed, with sewage ingress and vermin being major identifiable health risks, exacerbated by a recent downpour.

When Charlie reported on particular sites, including Mr Cuthbertson's 'Commercial Bank', it was clear that 'Cuthy' was uncomfortable. He tried to catch the eye of the Chairman, but that was focussed on Charlie. 'Cuthy' was running his chubby fingers around the inside of his starched batwing collar, as though needing to vent excess heat, and his lips bounced off each other in anticipation of speech.

Charlie continued, "The well in the basement of the 'Commercial Bank', after the recent inundation, was overflowing and flooding the premises. Fortunately, the flood water was predominantly fresh river water with little risk to health."

"How so sure that it was river water?" quizzed the Chairman.

Charlie replied, "When Mr McGregor and I went into the basement, we met Mr Cuthbertson who stood by the well with a large colander, full of brown trout. Fresh and lively they were too, Sir."

"McGregor, you are a conniving, snivelling, treacherous W… W…. Weegie," screamed Cuthbertson.

Jimmy mocked affront at this verbal assault and retorted, "As a true Glaswegian, 'snivelling', I must object to." His words were delivered, to general amazement, in tones as clear as a bell, straight from the foundry.

"Now, now, gentlemen. Through the Chair, please!" John Duncan pleaded.

Footnote:
Inspired by Minutes of the Blairgowrie Council c.1860. In advance of the installation of mains water to Blairgowrie, a bank basement was flooded. Fish were found swimming in the water. This perhaps contributed to the approval of that project. All names, etc are fictitious.

Designer

Jessie Nellies

I'm well on in years, near decrepit
And life's seemed to pass in a blink
Got a list of complaints like the others
But I'm not quite as deaf as they think.

That's why, "Mrs Posh" at the Gran's club
Doesn't know I heard every word
As I passed, I was scanned and recorded
Then she nudged her friend, quite disturbed!

"Just tell me how that woman does it.
That's another new coat she's got on.
Last week it was slacks and a jumper,
Then just in a flash, they'll be gone.

The silk suit she wore to the party
Was designer, I'm willing to swear
I bought one the same at the boutique
Which I'll struggle to pay off this year!"

Well, you're right, Missus, I'm on the pension
But I'm thrifty, for that I give thanks.
While you're worried sick paying plastic
I'm laughing right down to the bank

The slacks and the top came from Blytheswood.
The cancer shop, that was the coat.
And the fancy big bag from Barnardo's
Was "Fab, Mum" my dear daughter wrote.

So I keep on searching for bargains
To please everybody I've tried
To tell the truth I just love it.
If I don't get a rake, I'm deprived.

Should I ever need "something special"
You know where I'll make my first stop
I'm not paying designers a fortune
If there's one in the charity shop.

An Apple A Day

Jane Townsley

Deep in a hollow of the forest lived the seven dwarfs. Now that Snow-white had married her prince, they had more time for disagreements. The worst was when Happy discovered that Doc had no qualifications at all. He told Dopey and Grumpy.

"Then he's a charlatan," said Grumpy. "Not as much as a standard grade. He's got no more right to call himself a doctor than Dopey. I told you but no-one listens to me. Serves you right!" Grumpy stretched his long white beard in temper, before stomping off to bed.

"But... but I don't want to be a doctor," said Dopey fretfully.

"Don't worry. You won't be," Happy reassured him. "Go and fetch the others. We'll decide before Snow-white gets back."

"Snow-white's on honeymoon with Prince Charming. She won't be back until Wednesday. She said she'll bake us an apple pie when she gets here."

"It is Wednesday," laughed Happy. "Hurry up!"

Dopey jumped from the table and ran towards the door. "Hey guys," he shouted at the top of his voice. "We have to choose a new doc... Mmm..."

Happy slapped his hand over Dopey's mouth but it was too late. The other dwarfs had already stopped picking apples and were making their way towards the cottage.

"Is she here yet?" Sleepy asked.

"No, no," Happy said, thinking fast. "We need more sugar for the recipe. Would someone nip down to Tesco's?"

"I'm too tired," said Sleepy, stifling a huge yawn. "Must be all that apple picking." He had two apples in his basket.

"I... I... Aaachoo!" said Sneezy.

"Bashful, you go," ordered Doc, as he heaved his basket onto the table. "Snow-white said she'll only make the pie if I do the peeling. I've been looking forward to the pie all day but I hate peeling apples and she knows it!"

"I don't have any money," said Bashful, turning out his pockets. His face grew red with embarrassment.

"I have the perfect solution," said Happy. "The rest of us will peel the apples and Doc can go for the sugar. By the time you get back, Doc, all the peeling will be done."

"Eh? You'll peel *all* the apples?"

Happy nodded.

"But I don't know how," Dopey wailed. "And there's too many."

"You can practice on my two," said Sleepy.

"And.. and.. aachoo! And mine." Sneezy offered.

"That's very kind of you both," said Dopey, cheering up.

Doc was only too pleased to escape the dreaded apple-peeling.

"Don't tell Snow-white. Remember, if she asks, you're to say that I peeled all the apples. Got it?"

Happy nodded and the others solemnly swore an oath, promising never to tell, even if they were beaten and tortured on a roasting spit. Since Bashful, Sleepy, Sneezy and Happy were certain that Snow-white had never tortured anybody in her life, they agreed readily. Dopey wasn't sure but Happy prodded him hard with the wooden spoon and wouldn't stop until he gave in.

Finally, Doc was merrily on his way, no doubt thinking that he had outsmarted them once again.

Happy took charge. After he had explained the predicament, he announced, "Let's wake Grumpy up. He has a say in this".

"I'm already awake. How can I sleep with this racket?" Grumpy grumbled.

"When I burned my fingers, he packed them in snow until they cooled down," Sneezy offered.

"Maybe… but he didn't cure your cold, did he?" Grumpy said sarcastically.

"I don't think anyone can cure the cold," Happy said.

"I fell out of bed and stubbed my toe and he knew what to do," Sleepy jumped to Doc's defence. "And he put the bandage on properly."

"You don't have to be a doctor to bandage a toe," sneered Grumpy.

"I think he's awful nice," said Dopey. "I like him… lots… to be the doctor."

"That's not the issue, Dopey," Happy said kindly.

"Well, what is the iss… atchoo?" asked Sneezy.

"He isn't qualified!" asserted Grumpy. "To be a doctor, you must have a certificate and he doesn't. So we have to appoint a new doctor."

"But who?" asked Happy. "Let's put our heads together."

The six heads pressed to form a tight circle. One by one, they silently considered each other as potential candidates.

Grumpy was too… grumpy. He didn't have the right bedside manner. As for Dopey, well… if one wanted to survive, it wouldn't be sensible to choose him. Sleepy couldn't stay awake long enough to treat anyone and Bashful was too shy to look at his own body, never mind anyone else's. Happy was too cheerful - he would make jokes about their ailments and Sneezy might give them all the flu.

"Well, that's just fine and dandy," moaned Grumpy, pulling himself away and breaking up the group. "I might have known - there isn't a doctor in the house. Bah!"

"If we don't have a doctor, what'll we do next time one of us takes ill?" Sneezy panicked.

"Or if we're down the mine and someone has an accident? What then?" added Sleepy.

"I might… I might have… an idea," stuttered Bashful.

Everyone stared at him expectantly. He blushed.

"Well?" asked Sleepy.

"Yes?" asked Happy.

"I like ideas," said Dopey. "Is it a good one, Bashful? Ideas are..."

"Quiet," thundered Grumpy and Dopey fell backwards. "Tell us your idea. *Now!*"

Bashful looked as though he might burst into tears but he managed to stammer, "We... we could give Doc a certificate. That would make him a cert... cert... certified doctor."

"What a brilliant idea," gushed Happy. "A certified doctor.

My, my! That's as good as a qualified doctor. Let's do it."

Happy ran to fetch Bashful's sketchpad and calligraphy set and they got busy. They were just putting the finishing touches to the parchment when the front door opened and Snow-white and the Prince entered. She laughed as they showed her the certificate and even Grumpy cheered up when she agreed to sign it.

"I suppose if a princess signs it, it might be a real certificate," he conceded.

"It's a Royal Decree," added the Prince, "by appointment to Her Royal Highness, the Princess Snow-white. You don't get much better qualified than that."

"Now Doc's a real doctor," said Dopey with a grin.

"Of course I'm a real doctor," bellowed Doc from the open door. No-one knew how long he had been standing there. Snow-white giggled. "Of course you are, Doc, and all your friends have made you a certificate to prove it."

She rolled it into a neat scroll, then walking towards Doc, she announced, "Doctor Dwarf, I now present you with this certificate and declare that you are chief physician by special appointment to Their Majesties Prince Charming and Princess Snow-white. Congratulations."

She leaned over and planted a kiss on Doc's forehead. Immediately Doc's frown changed to a smile. Everyone laughed, even Grumpy. Doc placed the sugar on the table and unfurled the scroll.

"Aw shucks! Thanks, guys," he said and then added disdainfully, "But you can all go whistle if you think I'm peeling any apples!"

Driven

Catriona Ward Sell

i have been thinking about maps.

about where i have been,
and how ink places me
as i look each side of the motorway
for land

offpage, the mines and slides
are uninked,
a tea-ring victory, a torn misdirection,
an overworn page   where i should move on

i have been thinking about your house,
lying on the page, like
an unmarked police car: unnoticeable,
              lurking

i have been thinking about lines.
about how to draw them clearer
around the contours
of my body;

how to thickly outline myself
as an accident zone,
a do not cross,
an island

Yes,
I have been thinking about lines.
and everything that comes
in between them

And They All Lived Happily

Margaret Drummond

Some of you, like me, may have spent many hours of your adult life reciting nursery rhymes, firstly to your children and then perhaps to grandchildren. The traditional rhymes we all learned in childhood are stored in our memories just as surely as in any modern-day computer, ready for downloading and passing on to younger generations who, amazingly, still seem to enjoy them.

Years of looking after my small grandchildren may have sent my brain into nursery rhyme overload and I can't help but feel intrigued by the characters. What about the old woman who  lived in a shoe? I wonder how she got there? Why so many children? And why doesn't their father get a mention? After reading between the lines of "My Best Book of Nursery Rhymes", I think I can now reveal her true story - for adults only!

I reckon it all started with Georgie Porgie. When they were young, she was the one he kissed most often before the other boys chased him. The trouble was, she enjoyed his attentions too much, especially when he brought tasty pies to sweeten her up. One day, when the other boys were late coming out to play, one thing led to another and Georgie got her in the pudding club. The result was a baby girl named Bunting, born one cold winter morning. Georgie Porgie took one look at his new responsibility and ran out the door on the pretext of hunting rabbits to make a cosy cover to wrap Baby Bunting in. But he didn't come back and the single mum, Polly, moved in with her sister Sukey. This didn't work out as Sukey was jealous of the attractive Polly who often invited gentlemen callers in for tea and sympathy while Sukey was left holding the baby.

Soon, to Sukey's relief, Polly moved out to live with Jack Sprat whose lean and hungry looks turned her on. He was also known as Jack-be-nimble and had proved this to Polly by jumping out of bed, over a candlestick and through a window just as Sukey came running up the stairs to accuse her sister of burning the bottom out of another kettle. Jack turned out to be mean and kept Polly short of money. The birth of twins a year later put paid to rumours that Mrs Sprat had grown fat from overeating and was not feeding her husband properly, but by that time Polly was so fed up, she took the children and left Jack to his lanky lifestyle.

Polly again had the problem of finding accommodation for her brood until she met a property agent, an older man whose house was as bent as him - because he had skimped by employing cowboy builders. He offered her a peculiar property shaped like a shoe at a nominal rent, which was too expensive for Polly. He agreed to accept just sixpence a week, if she would supplement it by a substantial amount of tea and sympathy. Polly and family settled into Shoe-house and the arrangement continued until the agent got too decrepit to walk the crooked mile to her house every week. Polly was overjoyed and left the sixpence upon the crooked stile at the bottom of his garden until the old man got even more twisted at her rejection of him and took revenge by substantially increasing the rent.

By this time, there were four more offspring to support with no help from their crooked father, so a distraught Polly consulted a doctor called Foster because she didn't know what else to do. He was very sympathetic and hands-on, promising to take good care of her. He put Polly on the pill and she was under him for years until one stormy night in Gloucester when he stepped in a puddle right up to his middle and was never seen again.

After that, Polly started to get on her feet. Her children were grown up and making their own way. Bunting had married well and lived in nearby Banbury, visiting her mother often on her fine white horse to show off all the jewellery she charged to her rich husband's account. The twins were doing fine too. Mary, who was quite contrary but clever with it, pursued a career in landscape gardening whilst her brother Simon favoured the simple life and found casual work in fairgrounds.

Shoe-house actually belonged to a cobbler who had become tired of customers demanding fast shoe repairs for half-a-crown a time, so he opened a factory producing beach shoes that holidaymakers bought for a thong. The business earned him a fortune and he had moved to the Sandals resort in Spain, but now he felt homesick and decided he wanted his house back.

Polly refused to move. After all, she had lived there for so long and, although getting on in years, she was free of men at last and enjoying some independence. She had started taking HRT and didn't feel like an old woman anymore, more like a young thing. The cobbler felt like one too but couldn't find one. However, he  rather fancied Polly and, to her horror, threatened eviction unless she let him move in.

Poor Polly! She felt all stitched up again until she realized the cobbler wasn't rich at all, just a poor soul whose foot-loose lifestyle had left him down on his uppers with the house his only asset. So Polly devised a cunning plan and toed the line for a bit before overdosing him on so much tea and sympathy that she soon saw the boots off him. But not before she made sure she was left Shoe-house in his will.

Then she lived happily ever after.

Passing By

Jill Geary

Hearts and swallows fly
Against a cotton white
Cumulous backdrop

Where temporary wooden
Structures flash between
Tree tops of whip lash green

Sketching and tracing
On high blue bleeding through
To my white canvas soul

Bananas

Emily Copland

'She can't sack you for sawing a banana in half, Ruth. Come on down and have a cup of tea.'

I glowered at the closed bedroom door. 'No, thank you. I'll just get on with my revision.'

Outside on the landing, my mother sighed. 'It's not the end of the world, love. You'll get over it.'

Her footsteps clumped down the stairs and I was finally left on my own. I groaned with embarrassment as the replay of my very first day of employment flickered through my brain. How could I have made so many mistakes? I pulled the duvet over my head but the technicolour nightmare flashed on and on.

The box of tomatoes spilling across the floor between the feet of amused customers. The helpful hands returning their bruised and split corpses to me. The earwig making a bolt for freedom from the cabbages and up my sleeve. My terrified screams as I tried to shake it loose before it got to my ear. The punnets of mouldy raspberries that I had to sift through. The requests for stuff Id never heard of. If I had asked Stella once more to point out some unknown exotic veggie, she would have hit me with it. And then, to cap it all, those huge clumps of bananas that weighed a ton, and were home to poisonous frogs and spiders - so Stella assured me. I had to cut them into hands with a great sharp knife.

'Five or six to a hand, Ruth, quick as you can,' she said.
I was all fingers and thumbs. I managed four and a half, five and a half, six and a half bananas in a bunch, but couldn't avoid

sawing at least one of them in two. My only defence was that it was the way they were put together. If God had intended them cut into hands, they would have come with a dotted line and 'Cut here' printed on them. Why couldn't people buy thirty at a time? That's what I wanted to know.

The day juddered on from one disaster to another. I gave customers the wrong fruit, the wrong weight, the wrong change. I have never felt such a failure. At four o'clock, Stella led me through to the store, gave me a cup of hot chocolate, a biscuit and a box of hankies. The relief when she told me I needn't come back was wonderful. For a few seconds, it blotted out my feelings of total inadequacy. Stella wasn't terribly angry, but she did ask me to leave the hankies as she needed them as well.

I managed to walk home past all the competent members of the human race. I expected sympathy from my Mum. After all, she makes the odd mistake, but to see her trying to keep a straight face as I related my ordeal was too much to bear, so I retreated to my bedroom with as much grace as I could dredge up. I stayed there fretting till after six, getting hungrier and hungrier. Then the aroma of Mums lamb casserole wafted into my room. Funny that. She must have left the kitchen door open, and the door at the foot of the stairs. Hunger won over humiliation. I gave in to my growling stomach and went down.

'Ah Ruth, give us a hand, love, and make the custard, will you? You always make it better than I do.'

I suppose that's something I can do right, I thought, as I carefully measured out the milk.

'First job I had,' said Mum, 'I managed to spoil a whole bale of...'

'Hello there, the masters home, hungry, tired, wanting a bit of peace and quiet. Dinner ready? Smells good!'

I concentrated on making the custard and hoped Dad wouldn't ask about my disastrous day. Fat chance. He waited until I was trapped in my seat at the table before he began the interrogation. I looked down at my lamb casserole, hoping for inspiration. And it came to me. I had three options.

> a. Run to my room and hide for the rest of my life.
> b. Admit I made a few mistakes.
> c. Play to the gallery.

I played. I joked about banana splits, free-wheeling tomatoes, rotting raspberries. There wasn't a dry eye in the house.

Afterwards, Dad gave me a hug and slipped a tenner in my pocket.

'For the entertainment,' he said. 'Better than anything on the telly.'

When my friend Alison phoned later to find out how I had got on, I recapped the whole performance for her. Once we had calmed down, she told me about the vacancies for the new McDonalds that was opening. She was going to try for it. Did I fancy coming along? I thought about it for two seconds. After the greengrocers, McDonalds would be a walk-over.

'What, just serving chips? I could do that with my eyes closed. Let's go for it!'

We came, we saw, we conquered. Or at least we were accepted. Mind you, the job wasn't quite the walk-over that I expected. But that's another story...

Breakthrough

Elizabeth Leslie

The clock in the hall strikes eight as John strides down the drive. Emma watches from the window. Five minutes brisk walk and he'll be at the station. She imagines him greeting his fellow commuters, boarding the train then settling down to read his paper. An hour from now, he'll be starting another busy day at the office. So different from her day...

Last night's rain has stopped and sunshine floods into the room. Her heart wrings with despair. She wants to be out there too, doing all the things she used to do - walking, driving, shopping, meeting friends ... But that was when she was still the strong, capable one - the corporate wife, the busy mother of three boys and later the sole carer of two aging and difficult parents. And now, with her parents gone and the boys grown up and out in the world, only she and John are left - and the panic attacks which have turned her into a prisoner in her own home...

A burst of laughter from the television startles her. A handsome young chef is preparing a fruit pie on breakfast TV and showing the presenter how to plait strips of pastry to make a fancy lid. Perched on perilously high heels, she is giggling flirtatiously at him. With a mixture of envy and irritation, Emma grabs the remote and switches to the 24 hour news channel. Then she wishes she hadn't. They're re-running last night's big story from America - a man with a gun has run amok in a shopping mall. Terrified shoppers are blundering in all directions, their faces contorted with fear, their screams echoing in Emma's ears. With a shudder, she flicks the remote and the screen goes blank.

Glancing around her spotless and impossibly tidy living-room, she catches sight of her glum, defeated face in the mirror above the fireplace. What a contrast to the young, laughing girl in the wedding photo propped on the mantelpiece. She picks up the little wooden cat standing beside the photo, and strokes it gently. Her Christmas gift from Jack the year he was nine – proudly presented to her after hours spent in his bedroom whittling and carving. And now, ten years later, he's gone, the postcard from New Zealand his latest communication from his gap year travels.

Sighing deeply, she wanders into the kitchen, stacks and switches on the dishwasher, and deposits a shrivelled lemon in the compost bin. About to embark on yet another round of pointless cleaning, she pauses....

Through the window she sees the vibrant colour and life in the back garden. The garden she no longer ventures into.

Tears spring to her eyes. How she longs to feel the sun on her skin again, to walk on the soft springy grass. Can she do it to-day? Can she? A tiny flame of hope stirs in her. Tentatively, she opens the back door....

Immediately her heart starts to thud and her breathing becomes ragged. At the bottom of the garden the summerhouse seems to dance in the sunlight. Her grip on the door handle tightens. 'Breathe slowly, the panic will pass.' The familiar soothing words from her self-help CD play in her mind. Taking a deep breath, she steps outside. On trembling legs she ventures across the patio and down the path. There's a bee on the lavender bush. A blackbird watches her from the hedge. The delicate scent of sweet peas fills her nostrils and she smiles as she reaches out to touch the single raindrop lying on one soft petal.

Then, wobbly, but triumphant, she makes her way towards the summerhouse. She knows there's a long way to go, but she has just taken her first steps to freedom.

Generation Exit

Annie Johnstone

I sit here in my chair
My mind strolls back to a
Time when my opinion was
Still valid

Where conflict happened
To confront me not
Confound me or around me
Over me

The hustle and bustle of
The new generation waves
Goodbye to hard earned wrinkles
Mere redundant waste

10 Little Writers

Emily Copland

10 little writers, with contracts to sign,
1 read the small print, then there were 9.
9 little writers thought that they were great.
1 had his work reviewed, then there were 8.
8 little writers researching crime in Govan,
1 received a "Glesgae kiss," then there were 7.
7 little writers scribbling hard with bics,
1 got writer's cramp, then there were 6.
6 little writers hoping to arrive,
1 went on a writing course, then there were 5.
5 little writers trying not to bore,
1 failed completely, then there were 4.
4 little writers joined an agency,
1 reached 30, then there were 3.
3 little writers just wrote what they knew,
1 knew very little, then there were 2.
2 little writers, writing on the run,
1 lost his laptop, then there was 1.
1 little writer wrote Sci-Fi for fun,
the aliens abducted him, then there was none!

The Sandstone Head

Emily Copland

A feeling of pity
engulfs me
for his ravaged face -
blind, senseless,
rough with grains of sand.
No pupils
for those pitted eyes
staring out forever
on a changing world.
My hands are drawn
to the curve of cheek,
holding him like a lover,
warmth seeping
into his grainy pores -
but not
enough
to resurrect.

(Inspired by a poetry day at Perth Museum, when we got to
handle - with cotton gloves - relics from earlier times. In my
case, an early Celtic carving of a sandstone head).

Blairwriters (contributions in brackets)

Alan Adair spent his working life in the steel industry in Motherwell and London before retiring to Blairgowrie. Alan's interests are local history and deltiology (old postcards). (98)

Margaret Drummond has always "scribbled", but eventually developed her hobby into freelance work for business magazines. Now retired, Margaret enjoys writing in a more humorous vein. (113)

Jill Geary has written poems since she was a child, to express how she feels and how she experiences the world. Jill finds comfort and inspiration in poetry and hopes the readers of this anthology find the same. (41,117)

Heather Innes, folk singer and writer, is published in various Australian, Irish and UK magazines. Heather's autobiography "New Beginnings" is available from Lulu.com   (6)

Annie Johnstone is 24 and lives locally. She draws inspiration from local characters, scenery or snippets of information. Annie has lots of imagination and loves to play with words, as expressed in her poetry. (16,51,70,71,124)

Elizabeth Leslie joined Blairwriters over a year ago. Elizabeth has always enjoyed writing. She writes short stories and articles, some of which have been published in 'Scottish Memories' and 'Yours'. (31,39,79,88,95,121)

 Barbara Lynch, after 50 years, recently returned to Perthshire where she grew up. Barbara draws her inspiration from a lifetime of experiences. (13,34,78,91)

Susan Meldrum started telling stories to her brothers and sisters from as far back as she can remember. She gets inspiration from nature and the countryside around her home. (9)

 Janet McKenzie, past president of The Scottish Association of Writers, has poems, articles and fiction published in the UK and Scandinavia. Janet enjoys writing and discussing work with others. (7,14,58,62)

Jessie Nellies has lived in Blairgowrie all her life. Jessie draws inspiration from everyday situations and enjoys writing poems for friends and relatives. (21,43,73,104)

Born in Inverness, Rosemary Patterson studied Fine Art at Duncan of Jordanstone College, Dundee and now works as an artist / illustrator. She writes poetry in her spare time. (15)

Catriona Ward Sell recently moved to Leeds. Her poetry reflects a sense of place. She is unlearning words like loch and dreich and finding synonyms for "high rise council estate" and "loads of motorbikes". (76,84,86,112)

Jane Townsley, founder of Blairwriters, is published in various magazines and anthologies. Jane has won prizes in writing competitions, including SCDA One Act Festival. (18,23,36,45,53,106)

On-line members Emily Copland (118,125,126), Joy Dewar (30) and Dawn Mullady (82) have also contributed to this anthology.

Index

www.blairwriters.co.uk